1

GRADE A PUBLI(
P.O. BOX 18175
FAIRFIELD, OHIO 45018

This is a work of fiction. It is not meant to depict,
portray, or represent any particular real persons.
Character names, places, events, and dialogues are
products of the author's imagination and are used
fictitiously. Any resemblance to actual events or
persons, living or dead, is absolutely coincidental.

For information regarding special discounts on bulk
purchases, please contact Gradeapub@gmail.com.

Manufactured in the United States of America.

ISBN: 978-0-9852280-4-0

Cover design: Dynasty Covers Me
Editor: Cassandra Williams

INDIA WILLIAMS
P.O. BOX 18175
FAIRFIELD, OHIO 45018

ACKNOWLEDGMENTS

First and foremost, I must give honor to God for allowing me another opportunity to live my dream. I can't express the feeling I get every time I see my vision complete and brought to life. The cover makes it real, the edit makes it complete, but the readers make it worth it. There is so much gratitude in my heart for each and every one of you. Your support and encouraging words are unyielding and have been from day one. Thank you all from the bottom of my heart.

Without you, no one would know about The Real Hoodwives of Detroit; Gangstress; Dope, Death, and Deception; Still Deceiving; Money Over Everything, or Celebrity Wives Association. Please continue to rock with me and let's take this thing all the way to the top.

Love Always & Forever,

India

Prologue

"911, what's the emergency?" A chipper operator answered the call.

"I would like to report a double homicide."

"Excuse me, but did you say you're calling to report a double homicide?" The operator asked for clarification.

"Yes! Two people are dead." I said calmly.

"What's your location?"

"I'm at the Dell Hotel in room 616." I answered.

"Okay, stay calm. Police and emergency medical units have been dispatched. Help is on the way!" The operator sounded alarmed. "Are you in any danger?"

"No. Not anymore." I replied feeling the safest I'd felt in a very long time.

"Is the assailant still on the premises? Is he or she nearby?"

"Yes, she's here. As a matter of fact, she's so close, I can touch her." I said while placing the palm of my hand against the mirror.

"I'm going to stay on the phone with you until help arrives." The operator conveyed. "Help better get here fast before there's one more body added to the number." Dropping the phone into the sink, I placed the gun to my head, prepared to take what was left of my existence.

It seemed like yesterday when I was popping bottles and tags without a care in the world. Today, here I was contemplating suicide. I had everything or at least I thought I did until reality showed me that fame didn't come easy. The life of a celebrity wife is supposed to be all glitz and glamour. With red carpets, black cards, and tons of green money, who wouldn't want to be on the A-list? However, when the lights dim and the paparazzi fade, living life in the fab lane comes with a price. Some of us pay severely for our membership in the Celebrity Wives Association. Don't believe? Here's our Story.

Chapter One
Jasmine

"Pregnant! Are you sure?" I damn near screamed at Dr. Shiloh, my gynecologist.

"Jasmine, let's not act too surprised by this news." She rolled her eyes and wagged her finger in my face. "Come on now, we've been down this road too many times for you to be stunned." Dr. Shiloh was from India. Her English was excellent but her native tongue was still present and particularly noticeable.

"How did I let this happen?" I said more to myself than her. I'm sure she knew I wasn't speaking to her but that didn't stop her from chiming in anyway.

"Jasmine, they make condoms and birth control for a reason you know." Now Dr. Shiloh was my girl and all but she was beginning to piss me off. She had been my doctor ever since I was seventeen. She even delivered my son, Jordan. However, with the way I was feeling right now, if she kept talking, I was going to have to get ugly with her. This was not the time for speeches and I-told-you-so's. Right now, all I needed was a damn hug!

"Dr. Shiloh, please not right now, okay." I wiped at a tear that slipped down the side of my face. I was so disappointed in myself I didn't know what to do. This was my fifth pregnancy and would end up being my fourth abortion. Before you smack your lips and begin to judge me for what I've done. You should try asking me what my story is and where my pain comes from.

Life for me might appear to be glamorous to blog writers, magazine readers, and television viewers. But trust and believe, life for me is no walk in the park by most people's standards. My name is Jasmine James; I'm twenty-six years old and married to the hip hop legend, King James. No, not LeBron the basketball player from Ohio. My man was King James, the super hot, lyrical genius from the west side of Detroit.

Although King was his birth name, he went

by KJ for obvious reasons. He was a 6' 2" brother with light skin, beautiful teeth, wavy hair, and swag to die for. On a scale of one to ten, baby was at least an eleven. He got his break and was discovered about four years ago by Byron Washington, the CEO of Independent Records. After the contract was signed, King finally achieved fame and our lives changed instantly. Most people pray for shit like this. However, if I was being honest, this celebrity life is for the birds.

I longed for the old days when we shared a studio apartment, rode the bus, and ate McDonald's everyday. Crazy right? Well it's true. Money has changed KJ in the worst way. In some ways, I'm afraid it has changed me too. No, I'm not saying I'm siditty or anything like that. I still shop in the hood at the local malls and I can still chill in the cut and kick it with my people. What I'm trying to say is my standards have been lowered. Lately, my tolerance for King's bullshit is extremely high and that's not okay with me. I've watched him turn into my beautiful nightmare. I know I need to wake up, open my eyes, and walk away, but I can't; I just can't.

See, I've loved King since we were in Kindergarten. During recess one day, he asked me to be his woman, gave me a dollar, and a kiss on the cheek. I cried, took the dollar, and told the teacher. King got a time-out but he won my heart that day and has ever since. We were inseparable! He was my man and I was his bitch! Ride or die, I was by his side. After high school, he did some time upstate on a weapons charge. My mama wasn't feeling him but I had his back. I stuck out the three-year-bid with him and when he was released, I was standing at the front gate, arms wide open. It was then that he informed me that his new passion was rapping. I encouraged him to take action and pursue a rap career. Within months, his music ripped through Detroit like a virus. Eventually, other states began to take notice. Just like that, he was signed. Life couldn't have gotten any better. Or so we thought.

We soon discovered that I was pregnant and was given the news that we would be having a boy.

King was the happiest man in the world; he wanted everything to be perfect for our son. He got down on one knee and asked me to marry him right here in Dr. Shiloh's office. Of course, my answer was yes. Hence, we were married two months later. The lavish wedding, the exotic honeymoon, and purchasing our first mega-home was a breeze and no sweat off our backs. King had been signed for approximately six months by then. Money was flowing and everything was velvet. Actually, it was up until the night my water broke and our son, Jordan, was born.

Labor for me was extremely difficult. I felt as if I were dying. In my heart, I knew something was wrong. After Jordan was cleaned up and in my arms, I counted his ten tiny fingers and toes. I peered into both his beautiful, brown eyes and inspected his little ears too. Everything was present and accounted for but something was off. Staring at my son, it was then that I noticed he looked a little different from most babies and his cry wasn't normal.

Nobody said a word to me, not even King, my mother, or Dr. Shiloh. They all noticed it too but were afraid to say it aloud. The next day, Jordan was taken for a hearing test and his circumcision. About three hours later, he was returned to me with both good and bad news. The good news was he didn't have any hearing problems. The bad news was he had been diagnosed with Down syndrome.

After receiving that information, I was a mess. I blamed myself and cried constantly for my son. I was devastated that in less than twenty-four hours after coming into the world, he already had odds against him. King was crushed. Instantly, I began to feel a disconnection between he and I. Although he didn't admit it initially, he blamed me for Jordan's disorder, and that shit hurt like hell. How can you get through one of the most difficult situations in your life when the person holding your hand lets go?

He began to stay out late and party a little more. Within months, King was all over the Internet. He was rumored to have been with this model or that singer and even a few groupies. There was also mention of a few outside children, which as of yet, hasn't been confirmed. I never questioned him about the stories that I heard or read. Honestly, I didn't want to know the answer. All that mattered to me was that he provided for me and Jordan. It didn't matter that the rumors were probably true, because deep down, I knew he loved us. This was just his way of dealing with things. I didn't doubt his love at all. However, it did hurt my feelings that he rarely wanted to have sex when he came home from his tours.

On the rare occasions that we did get it on, he always used condoms. Fearing the worst like an STD or something, I asked him what the deal was. He admitted that he didn't want any more children. His rationale was because he was working all the time. Therefore, he didn't want me to have to handle two kids all by myself. I assured him that it didn't matter to me, that I would love to try again.

Aside from caring for Jordan and the occasional shopping trip, I wasn't doing much with my time anyway. He still refused; I was aware that it was because he didn't want another child like Jordan. I understood that most people couldn't deal with having a special needs child, so I backed off. We went back to using condoms. After one broke, I was told that I was once again expecting. King hit the roof and made me get an abortion. I didn't want to do it but my hands were tied. The same thing took place with the second unplanned pregnancy, as well as the third.

Every time I had to get on top of that table and kill a piece of me, I slipped further and further into a deep, dark, hole. I begged Dr. Shiloh to tie my tubes but she refused. "You're young! One day you will meet a man who wants to make beautiful babies with you and you will be sorry." She would say.

"Dr. Shiloh, I'm already married to King and he ain't going nowhere." I flashed her my rock as if she could ever forget him.

"He is no good for you and he is damaging your insides." She scribbled something down on a prescription pad. "Take this to the pharmacy, and I don't want to see you back here until your annual pap smear." She handed me the paper which was a prescription for birth control. "No more babies, Jasmine." Those were her famous last words.

That was four mouths ago. I was mortified to be sitting in her office with the same problem for the fourth time. "Jasmine, you are too smart to be so naïve. Please honey, at least keep this baby! "This may be your last chance at a normal pregnancy." She pleaded as I nodded. I wasn't saying I was going to keep the baby, but I did agree that this just might be my last opportunity. It would be wonderful to have another baby and prove to King that we could do it right. Unfortunately, I knew he wouldn't be a happy camper. "Jasmine, here are a few samples of prenatal vitamins. **IF** you decide to keep this one, start taking them as soon as possible."

Chapter Two

Tionne

I looked around the thirty thousand square foot California mansion in disgust. No longer could I see the beauty within this gated property. Gone was the love I once had for the home and its co-owner, my husband. Every painting on the wall and expensive piece of furniture was just another reminder of his bullshit.

"Tionne, where the fuck are you going?" Dallas looked over the marble banister. He was standing there in a pair of black, silk pajama bottoms. The oil on his chocolate brown skin was illuminated by the scented candles lined along the ledge. Every muscle in his chest and stomach area stuck out like a sore thumb. Dallas was a powerhouse! Had my husband not been one of the most famous rappers turned CEO of his own music label, he could definitely be mistaken for a professional bodybuilder.

"I'm leaving." I kneeled down to pick up the two pieces of Louis Vuitton luggage resting near my

Giuseppe-covered feet.

"You ain't going no where; especially with only two suitcases." Dallas chuckled. I even giggled a bit too. With all the clothing, shoes, and other worldly possessions upstairs in my closet, it did seem quite ridiculous to only be leaving with a few items. Even so, I decided long ago that if and when the time came to leave, I would only leave with whatever I'd come with. It was time for me to make my own way in life. I didn't want Dallas to take credit for anything, not even the labels across my round ass. "Come on baby, join me in bed and stop playing."

"Dallas, I'm serious." I had threatened more than two dozen times to leave his no good, two-timing ass. Each time I meant it but could never stay true to my word. It seemed as if he had an invisible hold on me; no one could see it but everyone knew it was there.

"Look, I'm not about to stand here all night. Quit playing and bring your sexy ass to bed." Dallas made his way down the semi-spiral staircase, taking each stair at a deliberately slow pace. I didn't have time for this nonsense tonight. He thought my threats were idle but he was gon' learn today. "You got another nigga or something?" Dallas teased me with a laugh. He knew I would always be his and so did I, or so I once thought.

"I should have another two or three. Hell, maybe four or five just to keep up with you." I said with my back to him.

"Ten niggas couldn't even love you like I do!" Dallas barked.

I could hear the flopping sound of his leather, house-shoes nearing. Without delay, my entire body tensed up. Every time I was prepared to walk away from him and his lies, he always found his way back in. The majority of the time, Dallas would apologize profusely for his behavior. Then he tried to make things better with a new piece of jewelry, an expensive new car, or a shopping spree. Sadly, he only got his act together long enough for me to let my guard down. Just when I thought my marriage would be okay, his ass would end up in the dog house again.

"Baby girl, did you hear me?" Dallas reached down to remove a piece of luggage from my tight grip. "I said I'm sorry; I love you."

"Dallas, you don't love nothing but pussy." I rolled my catlike eyes which were a mixture of hazel and gray–contacts of course.

"I can't argue with that." Dallas stroked his neatly trimmed goatee then rubbed a hand across his bald head. "If I didn't love pussy, I'd be gay."

"You know what I mean," I smacked my full lips. The MAC lip paint shimmered beneath the lights of the chandelier hanging in the foyer.

"Can't we talk about it?" His brown eyes peered into mine.

"Talk about what Dallas? This is hoe number fifteen!" I snapped. Normally, I was a quiet person until you pissed me off. "If you wanna talk about why that bitch was under your desk sucking your dick when I came to the office, then go ahead. Be my guest." Truthfully, she wasn't even the real reason I was leaving. Honestly, I was simply fed up with him period. I was tired of the way his forehead wrinkled when he smiled; I was tired of the way he left toothpaste all over the sink; I was tired of the way he slept at night; and I was tired of him always leaving the toilet seat up. More than anything, I was tired of taking chances with my life every time I slept with him. It was time that I had some much needed space. Catching him with this new bitch made leaving that much easier.

"I told you she was down there shining my shoes." He lied to me with a straight face.

"Oh, she was polishing something alright but it damn sure wasn't your shoes." I shook my head. Dallas was pathetic; his lies weren't even good anymore.

"You're jumping to conclusions. From your position at the door, it may have looked like my joint was in her mouth but it wasn't; I swear!" He raised his right hand as if he was taking an oath.

"Dallas, just shut the fuck up! There's nothing you can say or do that will persuade me to change my mind. I'm leaving and that's that."

"I thought you were in this shit for better or worse? 'Til death does us part, remember?" He tossed the wedding vows at me like they mattered. I had already endured the good, the bad, the ugly, and the most horrific shit imaginable. There were no more burdens for me to bear in this marriage. I was done!

"Dallas, don't bring up our vows. You and I both know they don't mean shit to you." Sighing from irritation, I stretched my neck to look past my husband. Through the stained glass surrounding our front door, I could see that it was raining cats and dogs outside. It made me reminisce about our wedding day many years ago.

The day was June 21, 2001, a Saturday afternoon at Hebron Sinai Baptist Church in Detroit, Michigan. Despite the protests of the then upcoming rapper, Black Bishop, aka Dallas Foster, family and friends had gathered inside the medium-sized church for our humble ceremony. By then, he had been in the music industry for about two years and felt that our wedding should have been a top-notch event rather than some average shit. I, on the other hand, wasn't for the glitz and glamour; I wanted my wedding to be eloquent yet modest, just as I was. See, I'm just an old-fashioned girl in love with being in love. Many of my girlfriends thought I had hit the jackpot when Dallas proposed. He wasn't the cutest man on earth. Then again, wealth made the nigga fine. They thought I only said yes for a paycheck but I swear on a stack of bibles, money had nothing to do with it.

"Well there's been a change of plans." Niles, my wedding planner announced as he entered the pastor's office. On that day, it was serving as a makeshift dressing room for me.

"What now?" I remember asking from the makeup chair. There had already been more catastrophes that morning than I wanted to count. First, my dress didn't fit and the flowers were wrong. Next, the ring bearer got sick then one of my bridesmaids got stuck in Florida after a layover flight.

"There's a severe thunderstorm headed this

way. I even heard mention of a tornado. I'm afraid the outside reception won't happen today, my love."

Niles rubbed my back. "I hate to stress my brides before their wedding about things I can fix. Regrettably, there's nothing I can do about Mother Nature."

"A tornado!" I shouted along with my mother and the makeup artist.

"Detroit doesn't have tornadoes!" Unwilling to except what he was telling me, I shook my head.

"There will be one today, love." Niles unbuttoned his suit coat and kneeled down beside me. "Police have asked everyone to remain where they are until this thing blows over."

"What does that mean?" Asked Toni, my mother.

"No one can leave here and more than likely, no one else will show up."

"Baby, maybe we should do this on another day." Toni said reluctantly. "I know how important today is for you baby girl but..."

"Mama, I know you have reservations but

this tornado can't last forever. We'll just have to wait." I replied on the brink of tears. I loved Dallas with every fiber in my being. He was my high school sweetheart, my first love, and my first sexual partner. Nothing would ruin my nuptials, not even some punk-ass tornado.

After two hours of unsuccessfully waiting for the storm to pass, there was a knock at the door. It was my mother again. "Hey pumpkin, are you feeling better." She closed the door and approached me where I sat on the pastor's leather loveseat. I remember being wrapped in a robe with rollers in my hair and a full face of makeup just staring through the picture window behind the pastor's desk. From my seat, she could see how dark it was outside. The trees were swaying from side-to-side, and I could hear the wind howling violently. Mrs. Bernie, the church secretary was running around trying to chase the huge hat that had just flown off her head. I wanted to laugh but my mood was somber.

"This is the worst day ever! Why is God

letting this happen to me?" I turned my attention away from the window to face my mother who was frowning. Thinking back now, I realize my question was upsetting. Toni had raised me to never question the works of God.

"Baby, I believe God is trying to get your attention." She took a seat beside me then cradled me in her arms. "Maybe this is a sign that you and Dallas shouldn't be joined in matrimony."

I remember being so angry back then, wanting to curse my mother out, but oh how true her words were. I wished I could tell Toni she was right. Sadly, she succumbed to breast cancer three years ago.

"What is wrong with you?" Dallas waved his hand in front of my face. "Have you been listening to me at all?"

"Look, I'm leaving. This time, I won't let you stop me." I snatched my luggage back from him.

"Where are you going? There's nowhere better than this!" He raised his arms in a God-like manner to indicate all the things I would be leaving behind. Dallas was a man of means. He knew most bitches would kill for the lifestyle he provided me. I'm sure he thought I was a fool to leave it all behind. "You have a twenty-four hour chef, a maid who cleans for you, and private yachts and jets at your disposal, yet you're leaving?"

"That don't mean shit if you can't be faithful! I spat. "I'm sick of you and your hoes Dallas. I can do better by myself and I will." As I made my way to the large door, Dallas couldn't prevent himself from tossing one more insult my way.

"Bitch, I made you!" He screamed. "I made your ass Tionne, from the teeth in your fuckin' mouth to those shoes on your goddamn feet!"

I stopped dead in my tracks at his startling revelation. Dallas had insulted me before but never on this level. As a child, my mother used to tell me that words would never hurt. To the contrary, that comment felt like an ass whopping for real. What hurt even more than his words, was the fact that he was right.

A natural beauty, I possessed brown skin, a few freckles, and sandy red hair. My body was well-proportioned with perfect D-cups, a medium waist, and an especially round ass. Sadly, once Dallas made it into the industry, I was no longer good enough. He turned me into what society considered to be pretty. My gapped teeth were covered with lumineers. My freckles were concealed with makeup; my beautiful hair was dyed coal black then stuffed with heavy extensions. Dallas also gifted me with a personal trainer. Although my frame was already nice, in a matter of months, I was sculpted into a stone-cold masterpiece.

Turning to look at Dallas, I smiled like a mad woman. "You're right D. You do own the shoes on my feet," so I slipped off the black, spiked wedges. "You also own the jeans on my ass," I said as I slid out of the spandex, Jessica Red jeans then tossed them at my husband. "I probably purchased this t-shirt with your money, so it also belongs to you." As I removed the top, Dallas reached for his dick. I'm sure my little striptease was right up his alley. The Victoria Secret bra and panties appeared to be painted on my body. He was turned on. Next, I removed the bob cut, black, lace front weave and tossed it to the floor. "Last but not least, you can have this too!" I was done living life according to Dallas.

"What are you doing?" He asked, no longer aroused but annoyed.

"I'm leaving!" I grabbed my luggage and chucked him the fucking deuces.

Chapter Three
Zuri Monae

As soon as the polar white, 2015, Mercedes Benz C300 with almond interior and chrome exterior pulled up to the stairs of the grand Victorian mansion, my stomach cringed. Without a word, I watched as Sturgis, our chauffer put the vehicle in park before stepping out to open our doors. Part of me wanted to grasp my door handle and hang on for dear life. However, it would've only delayed the inevitable. "Have a nice evening, Mrs. Armstrong." Sturgis looked almost apologetic for not prolonging the ride home from the preliminary boxing match that my husband had just lost.

"I'll be here at six a.m. sharp, Mr. Armstrong." Sturgis nodded at my husband before jumping back inside the whip and pulling off like a stunt driver in an action movie. Because I knew what was about to happen, my heart raced and panic set in.

"Come on sweetheart." Jason, aka "One-

Two", Armstrong, reached for my hand to assist me up the stairs. Standing six feet, my husband was stunning with perfect chocolate skin, ultra white teeth, and a deep dimple in his chin. Additionally, he was charismatic and could charm the panties off anyone with a vagina. To the world, I had done well for myself by locking him down. Conversely, only Jason and I knew the monster he could become given the right situation or circumstance.

With a smile yet trembling, I placed my hand into his and ascended the stairs. The silence was deadly as we walked up thirteen cobblestone steps toward the front door. I counted each one to take my mind off the misery yet to come.

Upon entrance into the quiet home we shared with our infant daughter, I watched as Jason removed his Armani suit jacket then the big face Oyster, 48mm, Rose-gold Rolex covered in diamonds. Casually, he laid the piece of expensive jewelry I'd given him after a big win last year on the foyer table then tossed his jacket atop it. "Baby, you did really well tonight. Those judges were stu..." I never got the chance to complete the sentence before Jason balled up his massive fist and punched me right in the stomach. Naturally, I doubled over in pain. That's when he came with an uppercut to my chin sending me stumbling backwards. "Stop it! Jason, stop it please!" I screamed for all of California to hear me. No matter how many times this occurred, I never could get used to the pain.

Wrapping his hand around my throat, Jason lifted my almost anorexic frame off the floor. Although I stood nearly six feet tall, only the tips of my toes could touch the cherry oak floor. "Please!" I begged but Jason was in a zone. Anytime he lost a preliminary fight or experienced any type of disappointment in life, he sent blows and body shots my way. Although his hands were registered in all fifty states as lethal weapons, he continuously used me as a punching bag because he knew I would take it and wouldn't dare call the police. Why would I? Calling the police on him meant tarnishing his reputation. A tarnished reputation didn't put food on the table. Ultimately, it took money out of my household. Yeah, I know you're over there in disbelief at what I said but I'm just keeping it one hundred.

As a thirty-five year old, five division world champion, the 1996 silver medal winner of the Olympics, and undefeated heavyweight boxer in his class, my husband was worth well over nine hundred million dollars. He was a big deal with several endorsements as well as his own sports representation agency. The life that Jason provided me outweighed his temper tantrums.

"Stop that shit right damn now!" Sylvia, Jason's mother, yelled from the top of the stairs. She was peering over the railing with a disapproving look. "Jason Renaldo Armstrong, what in the hell has gotten into you!?"

"I lost my preliminary match." Jason stopped battering my body then turned toward his mother. I tried to pull myself together; however, my bearings were off due to the lack of oxygen.

"Lost what…your got damn mind, that's

what!" Sylvia flew down the steps to assist me.

"Zuri, do you want me to call for help?"

"No!" I screamed. "No police. I'll be fine." I nodded before collecting the Alexander McQueen's that had come off my feet during the beatdown.

"She'll be fine mama." Jason briefly glanced at me before climbing the stairs dismissively. That was his ritual. He would beat the snot out of me then lock himself in the bedroom so he wouldn't have to see what he'd done.

"Is Jelly asleep?" That's what we called my daughter Angelica.

"Been sleep for hours." Sylvia stood in the middle of the foyer with both hands on her hips looking puzzled. "Why are you acting like you just didn't take an ass whooping from a professional boxer?" Sylvia lived in New York. Therefore, she had never bore witness to her son's rage. Currently, she was in town to visit for a month to help care for Jelly. I was thankful she was here to stop the violence, especially tonight.

"This ain't nothing new; just leave it alone

Syl." Although the right side of my face was lumped up, I tried as best I could to smile.

She grabbed my arm and whispered, "How long he been beating on you?" I started not to reply because it was none of her business, but I knew my mother-in-law wouldn't let it go, so I gave in.

"You remember his twenty-sixth birthday party? The one you threw him in Hawaii and invited everybody." I looked on as she recalled the event.

"Yeah. That's when his punk-ass daddy 'missed' the flight and didn't make it." Sylvia made air quotes with a frown. "Jason was so angry."

"That's when it started."

"That was nine years ago Zuri! Why haven't you put an end to this? I know that's my son, but his ass needs to be dealt with for putting his hands on you. You need to call the police." Sylvia urged.

"I can't call the police on him, Syl. Jason and Jelly are all I have in this world." With those words, I limped up the stairs.

"Zuri Monae!" Sylvia called out in a mother-like, yet scolding manner. I turned to face her. "Look at you. You're a stunning supermodel with your own awards and accolades. Baby, you have to learn to love yourself more than you love my son." Sylvia thought she was dropping knowledge on me. However, I wanted to tell her that love had nothing to do with it. Money meant power and cash was king in my world.

Born and bred in the slums of Kingston, Jamaica, I had endured far worse for much less. I'd overcome being beaten by my grandmother, raped by my uncle, and abandoned by both of my parents. Yep, that's right my father, Nada, and my mother, Bambi, left ya girl when I was only two years old to head for the United States. Their intentions were to secure work and living quarters then send for me. But you know how the story goes, they got caught up in the ways of the world and never looked back.

Day in and day out, I would watch the mail with hopes of a letter from the U.S. After several years of waiting, I learned that I was all I had. I made a vow that no matter what, I would leave the slums and head for higher ground. True to my word, at the age of twenty-two, I used my silky skin and long legs to catwalk out of the ghetto. America had been good to me but Jason had been even better. Life was great, aside from his periodic bullshit. At least now I had tissue dipped in 24 karat gold to catch my tears which is more than I can say for other women in my situation.

Chapter Four
Diamond

Buzzz. Buzzz. Turning on my side, I grabbed the iPhone and answered, "Hello."

"Happy b-day sis!" Dexter, my older brother, yelled into the speaker.

"Thanks bro." I turned the volume on my phone down to drown out the noise in his background. It sounded as if he was at a party.

"Girl, it's early. I know you ain't sleep."

"Yeah, I was. I had a long day," I yarned.

"Doing what? Shopping and spending money?" He laughed.

"No nigga, I was working!" I snapped.

"I'm sorry; I didn't know conning men out of their money was such a strenuous occupation." He retorted.

"The fuck you mean!" I cut into him for trying to hoe me.

"Look, I didn't call to start no shit. I was only calling to wish you happy birthday."

"I'll call you tomorrow. Be safe out there." I said before ending the call and dropping the phone down. Although I wanted to be pissed off with my brother, how could I? He was right. Not long ago, conning men and running scams was my full-time job and I was good at what I did. You can think what you want but a bitch had to eat. This poor girl from the projects managed to hustle her way up to penthouses and Porsche cars.

You see, after administering all the game I could on the male residents of St. Louis, I packed my shit and headed to Hollywood. I knew the money was in Tinseltown and I was bound to eventually snag an actor or a Beverly Hills surgeon. I landed a job at an exclusive exotic dance club in Melrose and immersed myself with the "in" crowd. Before long, I was going on dates with musicians, producers, and the like. It felt good to be arm candy until I realized it was time to secure a future. I no longer wanted to be a fling, weekend thing, or a jump off. It was time to become a wife. Unfortunately, I didn't have any prospects until a chance encounter with my new boo, Kensington Tucker, who was the starting shooting guard for the Los Angeles Lakers.

The night we met in Los Angeles at a twenty-four hour diner on La Cienega Boulevard was purely coincidental. I'd gone there to pick up a steak and lobster meal after leaving the strip club, and he was dining with an entourage. The place was packed. Therefore, I had to stand in line for nearly thirty minutes waiting on a table before I was finally granted access into the diner. Upon entrance, I spotted the famous NBA star at the table shooting the breeze with his squad. He was larger than life and finer than I recalled him being on television.

Without a word, I made my way past his table then sat down in my booth. From my position, I could hear all the chatter between him and his friends. His smile was captivating and his laugh adorable. I remember seeing an interview with him during playoffs; he seemed to be very humble and kind. You don't find that these days with professional athletes. Because of that, some way–

some how, I had to make my mark on Ken. Regrettably, from my position, I could also see several obstacles in my way–they were called groupie bitches. Several of them surrounded the table of men, practically falling over themselves to get an autograph or a picture. Some of them were cuter than me and slimmer than my size eight. Nonetheless, I one-upped the competition by calling Ken's waitress.

"Oh I'm sorry; I'm not the waitress for this section, she's on her way though." She said.

"I would like to pay his bill." I pointed to the table full of food and beverages.

"There are twelve people on his tab, are you sure?" She frowned. "His bill is almost one thousand dollars."

"I got it." Without worry, I reached inside my Birkin bag then placed ten, big face Franklins in her hand.

"I'll let them know." Bewildered by my actions, she stepped away. As I placed my order with my own waitress, I watched as Ken's waitress delivered the news. Every man at the table strained their eyes to see who had just dropped a grand on their meal. When Ken's eyes met mine, I simply nodded. I realized my move was bold but it paid off.

Within minutes, Ken made it his business to introduce himself to me. The two of us chilled for over an hour. By the end of the night, Ken walked away with admiration and appreciation for an independent woman such as myself, and I walked away with his digits. We chatted every day thereafter; and within three months, he asked me to be his girl. That was six months ago. Since then, I've been trying to stay on the straight and narrow. I had it good with Ken and I planned to rock with him until the wheels fell off.

"Happy birthday to you…happy birthday to you…happy birthday Diamond, soon to be Mrs. Tucker…happy birthday to you." Speaking of Ken, he barged into the bedroom wearing nothing except an apron, a pair of Jordon's, boxers, and a chef's hat. He was carrying something covered by a bronze lid on a tray with fancy silverware, a linen napkin, and a small vase with a red rose.

"Aww snap! Don't tell me you been down there cooking for a sistah?" I sat up in the twelve foot, circular, custom bed and hit the light on the nightstand.

"I'll do anything for my baby especially on her birthday." Ken displayed the contagious smile that made me fall for him almost nine months ago.

"Thank you baby, but what is it?" I looked over at the tray cautiously. I had never known Ken to cook anything, so I was a little scared.

"Girl, this here is the joint." He lifted the lid and steam hit me in the face. When the smoke cleared, I was in awe of the culinary masterpiece before me.

"Baby, you did not bake this chicken, candy these yams, or cook this macaroni." I shook my head.

"I did too and I got the dishes downstairs to prove it." Ken sat his lanky, six foot seven frame down on the bed beside me. "I had to call in the big guns to pull this off."

"You called your mother." I replied already knowing who the big gun was.

"Yeah, I Skyped her and she talked me through the whole thing." Ken admitted. "She said she has to meet the woman who has me in the kitchen because she must be special."

"Is that right?" I grabbed the gold fork and dug into my food.

"I told her we'll set-up something soon with the whole family."

"You must be feeling ya girl if you're trying to take me home." I smiled at my man. Although he was twenty-six and covered in tattoos with tons of facial hair, Ken possessed a baby face and boyish good looks.

"Hell yeah, I'm feeling you. If I wasn't, you wouldn't be here." With a chuckle, Ken stood from the bed.

"Where are you going?"

"I have to clean up the kitchen."

"Let the maid do it bae." I whined. He was only in town for a few more days until he returned

to Denver for training camp. Consequently, I
wanted to spend every minute with him.

"She doesn't come back until tomorrow.
Besides, your nigga is a neat freak." Ken was right.
In his condo, everything had a place. His walk-in
closet was organized to a tee. All of his clothes were
categorized with an area for sportswear, casual
wear, and special events. All four hundred pairs of
his shoes were in plastic containers with a picture
on the front so he would know what was in each
box without removing the lid. Even his jewelry
section looked like the display counter at Diamonds
International. "On my way downstairs, I'll run you
a bath." Ken called out before entering the
bathroom in the guest suite that I slept in.

"Will you come back up and join me?" I
asked seductively.

"You know I can't Diamond." Ken was
super religious in regard to abstaining from sex
before marriage. He told me he believed his
faithfulness to God's word was what allowed him to
be blessed in his NBA career. The brother was super

successful and hella paid, so I couldn't argue with his theory. It was however, hard to play my position. I'm not gon' lie, a bitch had needs. Many of nights, I contemplated stepping out. Then again, I knew I couldn't afford to lose Ken on account of some random dick so I played cool. Furthermore, I had a feeling my ring was coming real soon. Until then, I would continue paying the "good girl" Ken thought I was.

Chapter Five
Lyric

"Mom, my teacher said you haven't paid my tuition yet so I can't go on the fieldtrip tomorrow." Leslie, my 12-year-old daughter said after joining me in the kitchen. With my eyes wide, I continued scanning the contents of the refrigerator as an attempt to conceal my facial expression from my child.

"I was thinking about doing some fish and shrimp tacos for dinner. What do you think baby?" I asked nonchalantly.

"Mom, did you hear what I said?" Leslie took a seat atop the barstool resting in front of the counter. "My teacher said you haven't paid my tu..."

"I heard you." I closed the sub-zero, stainless steel refrigerator doors then turned to look at my daughter. "Some things came up baby and mommy had to push some bills around. I promise I'll pay it next week."

"Ok." Leslie sighed.

"Where is the fieldtrip going to be?" I knew my daughter was disappointed. Leslie was a good kid who barely asked for anything. I felt like shit to not be able to send her on this trip.

"We were going to the California Science Center." Leslie was a scientist in the making; she loved everything about chemistry, biology, and formulas. This meant she was heartbroken to not be going to the one place she had her heart set on all year. "It's okay, maybe you and dad can take me this summer." With a shrug, Leslie turned to leave the kitchen.

"Hold up baby. Grab the checkbook out of my purse."

"Thank you mommy! You're the best!" Leslie flew to retrieve the checkbook and was back in no time. I really couldn't afford the twelve thousand dollars for school tuition right at this moment but it didn't stop me from writing the check like it was nothing. *By the time they cash this, I should have money in the bank,* I thought to myself. Writing a bad check was a daring move that could've landed my ass in jail but dammit my baby deserved to see the fucking science center.

"Go put that in your book bag then finish that homework" With a smile, I watched my daughter skip happily away. It felt good to be able to save the day but I also felt terrible for committing fraud. "The storm won't last forever," I mumbled before returning to the task of making dinner.

RINGGGG. RINGGGG. "Hello," I greeted after grabbing the phone from its wall-mounted cradle in the large chef's kitchen with bronze and brown backsplash and matching butcher block countertops.

"Care to comment on your husband's drug habit, Lyric?" A voice heckled on the other end.

"Don't call my house again!" Flustered, I ended the call.

"Who was that bae?" Damien, my husband of eleven years called from the dinning room. He was sitting there reading a script his agent sent by carrier this morning.

"Nobody." I lied while holding back tears.

"Well why are you crying?" Damien entered the kitchen, wearing nothing except a pair of Hanes pajama bottoms and a smile. His golden dreadlocks hung over his shoulders and his hazel eyes sparkled in the light.

"Those tabloid people keep calling the fucking house and it's pissing me off!" I had already changed our number five times. It was supposed to be unlisted but somehow those fuckers just kept on calling. "I'm tired of this Damien," I confessed.

"I know baby; I promise it will get better soon." Damien pulled me into his embrace and held me, allowing my tears to wet up his chest.

"When Damien!?" I shouted; my ass was furious. "The fucking bills are past due; the bank is trying to take our house! We can't even afford to pay attention! So tell me when it's going to get better!?"

"Screaming isn't going to make the situation better." Damien tried to remain calm. He understood that I was hurting and it was all because of him, but I guess he didn't want the kids to be alarmed. "We'll figure this out."

"I'm tired Damien; I don't have anything left." I was done with being the resolution expert for everybody in my damn life. The pressure was unreal. Sometimes I just wanted to go to sleep and not wake up but I knew my children depended on me. "I didn't create this mess, you did! So you fix it!" Pulling back, I wiped my eyes and walked away. As Damien watched silently, I knew he wished he could go back to when life was simple, when we were just two poor kids growing up in Boston. Money and fame had complicated things to no end. Life had taken a turn for the worse. Damien recognized that I was at my breaking point, praying for a breakthrough before it was too late.

Slipping into the guest bathroom on the main floor, I flopped down on the toilet and cried hysterically. I turned on the water to mask my sobbing. Apparently, it didn't work because within ten minutes, there was a knock on the door. "Mom, are you alright in there?" Jonah, my 8-year-old son asked.

"I'm fine baby. I burned my hand that's all." I lied.

"Want me to get you some ice?" Jonah called out.

"No, I'll be alright baby; just give me a minute okay?"

"Okay. I love you; I hope you feel better." Jonah was a sweetheart by nature.

"I love you too." I said while suppressing the sound of my cries. However, now the tears flowed even quicker than ever. I loved my children with everything I had but sometimes, I wanted to give up. My shoulders had been carrying a heavy load for quite sometime and I was beginning to feel defeated. "Where did we go wrong?" I asked the question aloud although I already knew the answer.

Nine years ago, Damien and I were on cloud nine. His first sitcom had just been picked up for national syndication. He had also landed a movie role with some of Hollywood's vets. From there, his career took off. Before either of us knew it, we were chartering private jets around the world. Our money flow appeared to be never-ending and struggling was a thing of the past, until addiction showed up and showed out.

Four years into living the good life, Damien felt the pressure to experiment with some Hollywood friends and cocaine. Soon enough, he was addicted. At first, I paid his habit no mind. Hell, I was too busy enjoying my newfound fame and fortune to pay attention. Being young and naïve, I had even dibbled and dabbled a few times with him. Thank God I didn't form an addiction but the same could not be said for Damien. Initially, I thought my husband was only going through a phase. However, I soon learned otherwise.

After a few run-ins with police and several tantrums on movie sets, Damien found his way into the unemployment line. No one wanted to do business with him. As a result, our bank accounts took a nosedive. Nonetheless, in spite of his downfalls and shortcomings, I remained by his side.

I started a celebrity styling business to keep funds coming in. With my connections in the industry, the company took off and was doing numbers. Things were looking up for my family until one of Damien's last bouts with drugs.

As a result, I ended up spending a great deal of money on Damien's treatment as well as bribing the media to keep it on the hush. I realized it was a gamble when I invested in his sobriety. Even so, it was a risk I was willing to take to save my husband. Unfortunately, the gamble didn't pay off. Damien couldn't even stay clean for six months. For that reason, all of our accounts were in the red. My company was practically bankrupt. Eventually, everyone would know my business–family, friends, and the world. I wasn't ready to face the music and prayed like hell I didn't have to.

Knock. Knock. Again, someone was pounding on the door. "Jonah, mommy is fine." I turned the water off and stood.

"It's me Lyric," Damien sighed. I wanted to tell him to get lost but I couldn't. Damien was the love of my life. He was my everything. I couldn't turn my back on him no matter how bad I wanted to.

"I have this new script Lyric. We're gonna get back on top." Damien's voice seeped through the space at the bottom of the bathroom door.

"I hope so, Damien." With tissue in hand, I emerged from my sanctuary. "I really hope so."

Stepping into the hall, I took a quick look around the urban contemporary mansion with gold posts and marble floors. In a matter of sixty days, my beautiful home was going to become property of the bank. I hadn't paid the mortgage in almost a year. It wasn't due to neglect; I simply just couldn't afford it. Our house payment was a whopping thirty grand a month. Add that to the children's private school tuition, car notes, other bills, groceries, as well as both mine and Damien's parents' mortgages, I was almost two million dollars in debt. The sum once sounded like pennies to us young millionaires. Now a bitch was practically counting pennies to keep the lights on and food in the fridge.

"Just have faith in me." Damien pleaded. "I know I'll land this one."

"I have faith Damien." I lied with a straight face, only saying what he wanted to hear because that's who I was. What I wanted to tell him was my faith in him died the last time he snorted a line of cocaine.

On the other hand, I did have faith in myself. The last few years had been rough but I had a few tricks up my sleeve. This hood chick from Boston still knew how to make a dollar out of fifteen cents. Where I came from, only the fittest survived. Dammit, I was a survivor–always had been, always would be.

Chapter Six
Jasmine

I grabbed the prenatal vitamins that Dr. Shiloh had left atop the counter, looked at them then tossed them into my purse. Next, I slid on my black, spandex pants, and pulled up my tan and brown Coach rain boots. I gave myself the once over in the large mirror that was hanging on the wall. Staring at my reflection, I wondered why I felt so ugly and empty inside. According to most people, I was a pretty girl. My skin tone was that of creamy caramel. My eyes were almond shaped and my lips were full. I was 5 feet 4 inches and weighed a sexy, one hundred and forty pounds. Had I been a little taller, I probably could've been a model. But right now, I felt like a rag doll.

Blinking rapidly, I shook the somber mood off. I had to pull myself together. Therefore, I said a quick prayer, grabbed my gold LV bag and was out the door in seconds. I blew through the pastel pink lobby that was full of women with my head buried down in my purse. My long, Malaysian hair extensions covered the sides of my face as I pretended to be searching for something. I was not trying to be noticed by a KJ fan who recognized me from a television special or magazine spread. I was also ducking the paparazzi who made it their business to be all up in my shit everyday, all day.

Now that KJ was famous, my life had become an open book and I didn't need any attention today, especially not up in the fucking gynecologist's office. "Hey girl, where did you park?" I called my best friend, Stacy, as I scanned the parking lot for her cranberry colored Chrysler 300. She was acting as my assistant and chauffer for the day.

"Damn bitch, put your glasses on. I'm right here in front of the door." She laughed; I laughed too because she was indeed parked less than ten steps away from me. I hustled over to the car and gave her the middle finger. Her dumb ass was leaning on the car horn and people were starting to stare at us.

"Stace, cut that shit out." I laughed.

"They say if you can't see, then you must definitely be able to hear. I blew the horn so that your blind ass could find your way to the car." Stacey started up the car then pulled out of the parking lot. We rode in silence for about eight minutes until Stacey spoke again. "Damn, what's wrong with you?" She asked as we merged unto the 696 freeway.

"You already know." I rolled my eyes because I knew she was about to go ham on my ass. Stacy wasn't your average friend; this bitch keeps it one hundred even when you don't want her to. We've been friends ever since middle school and I love her like a sister. She was my main bitch for real.

"Jasmine, don't tell me you're pregnant again." She shook her head with a disappointed expression plastered on her face.

"Alright then I won't." I shifted in my seat. She looked over at me in disbelief. Out of shame and embarrassment, I looked away.

"Fuck that Jas! You are definitely having this muthafuckin' baby. Your ass can't keep getting abortions girl. King is just going to have to understand." Her mind was made up for me. I wished it was that simple but it wasn't.

"You know how King feels about more babies." I said getting choked up because I really did want another child.

"Fuck King!" She shouted, causing me to jump slightly. "It ain't like that nigga is even home anyway, and when his ass is home, he doesn't ever kick it with Jordan. You could be out here getting loose with his money like some of the other hip hop wives we know. They're out asking for liposuction, tummy tucks, cars, and houses. Shit, all you want is a damn baby! It seems to me that he shouldn't mind having another child if it's something you wanna do. I mean, it ain't like y'all broke and can't afford it. Hell, even broke niggas in the hood be having 'bout six...seven kids, trying to dodge child support like the police." She laughed. Just then my iPhone vibrated. "Hello." I answered without peeping the caller ID.

"What up Jazzy; where you at?" King spoke loudly into the phone. There was a bunch of noise in his background. I could tell he was at the airport. They were calling gate numbers and announcing delays over the loudspeaker.

"I'm in the car with Stacy; what's up?" I put my index finger inside my free ear so that I could hear him better.

"I told you 'bout hangin' with that bitch; you gon' listen one day." He smacked his lips. I glanced over at Stace to see if she had heard him. Her expression didn't change, so I kept on talking.

"Where are you baby?"

"I'm at the airport in Dallas. Something happened with the jet. They're working on it, but it won't be fixed until tomorrow. I told the label that I was ready to get the fuck home, so me and D-Bo 'bout to hop on the next thing smoking back to the D."

"Yay!" I squealed. My man had been on location at a movie set for the past five months. I had only saw him approximately six times during that entire stretch, so I was anxious. "Baby, what time does your flight land? I want to be at the airport with Jordan to pick you up."

"Damn baby, I'm on standby. I don't know what time I'll be home because I don't know what flight I'm leaving on…" He paused, "I'll just see you when I get there and you better have that pretty pussy trimmed up and waiting for me."

"You know I keep my shit tight all the time." I giggled and Stacy rolled her eyes.

"I know you do Jazzy; yo' shit is on point! That's why you're my wife. Now go buy yourself something sexy and I'll see yo' fine ass sometime tonight."

"Love you." I blew a kiss through the phone then ended the call.

"Ugh." Stacey gagged.

"What?" I asked my girl who was giving me the screw face.

"Nothing girl. Don't mind me and my disdain for your nigga." She waved a dismissive hand and shook her head. I hunched my shoulders, reclined back in the seat, and closed my eyes before I said something I would later regret.

Although I knew Stacey had my best interests at heart, sometimes I wished she would stay out of my business. A lot of outsiders viewed Stacey as a hater but I knew otherwise. She had no reason to hate because she was a beautiful girl who resembled the model Tyra Banks–smile, skin tone, height, and all. The men in the music industry flocked to her whenever she attended an event with me. I know for a fact that she had gotten down with a few of them and even still remained fuck buddies with at least one on the YMCMB label. Hate wasn't the reason she disliked KJ and I knew it. Stacey has been my girl since way back and has played witness to the good, bad, and ugly shit happening in my life. She was always my shoulder to cry on after fights with King. She also lends me her ears when I need a sounding board. All in all, she was my dog. I just wished she would lighten up on King.

"So I guess you aren't hanging with me and

Tracey tonight like you promised." Stacey reminded me, causing my eyes to pop open. I had completely forgotten that tonight was part one of Stacey and her twin sister, Tracey's, birthday celebration. Today was actually her sister's birthday being that she was born at 11:59 p.m. Stacey was born the next day at 12:01 a.m. For that reason, they always had a two day celebration.

"Damn Stace, I totally forgot just that quick." I felt awful; I knew she thought I was putting her off for my man, once again.

"It's cool, don't even worry about it." She brushed me off.

"Stace, don't play me like that. You know I haven't seen King in a while. Truth be told, you would do the same in a heart beat if one of those thugs you was fucking with went to jail for a stretch and was finally coming home." I smiled and Stace did too. She knew I was right.

"Whatever bitch." She flipped me the finger and I blew her a kiss.

"You know what Stace, I might just have a

plan."

"I'm listening." She cut on her blinker to signal her left turn.

"King doesn't know what time he'll get home. It will probably be late. I'm going to come to the party then leave a little early and be home before he gets back." When I said that, she smiled. "Now before you go getting all happy and shit, remember I probably won't be at your party tomorrow night. It all depends on how King is feeling." I warned so she wouldn't act brand new if I didn't show up.

"Okay, that's cool. As long as you can party with me tonight, it's all good." She said then turned up her sound system. We bumped the new August Alsina album all the way to Tracey's house.

BEEP. BEEP. Stace blew the horn and out popped Tracey on the phone looking ghetto fabulous. Tracey's ass was a bona fide hood rat. Yet, she somehow managed to acquire and maintain some really nice things. For instance, this girl hasn't had a job in a month of Sundays but she was driving a 2014 Jaguar. She lived in a plush townhome in a newly developed subdivision and her gear was always fresh to death. "Trick, stop blowing; I hear you. I got neighbors." She called to her sister then turned around to lock her front door.

"Hey Jasmine, can I hold a dollar?" Tracey's 8-year-old son, Prince, approached the car with his hand out. I smiled at the little handsome boy who was the spitting image of his mom.

"Oooh, me too! Can I get a dollar?" Princess, Tracey's 3-year-old daughter, asked. Reaching inside my purse, I was about to hand both of them a five dollar bill. However, Tracey pulled them away from the car with an attitude.

"What I tell y'all about asking people for their money? Get in the car with grandma." She scolded as she ushered them toward a grey Ford Focus that was parked in her driveway.

"I didn't know your mom was over here. Let's get out and speak to her," I suggested to Stacey.

"You go ahead, I'm good. That old bitch

ain't trying to talk to me." She smacked her lips.

"Damn, why you say that?" I asked with my hand on the door handle.

"She always has her damn hand out that's why. I work too hard for mine, so I don't put nothing in her greasy palms. Somehow, Tracey gets her money easy and she keeps my mom happy. Needless to say, my mama is team Tracey all the way." Stace rolled her eyes.

I nodded my understanding and stepped from the car. I walked up to the door of the Focus and tapped lightly. "Hey mama." I said as she opened her door and stepped out for a hug.

"Hey Jasmine, look at you." Her voice was raspy like Frankie's, Keyshia Cole's mother. "You still look good girl. That man of yours still rapping?"

"Yes ma'am." I smiled.

"Is the money still right?" She winked.

"Uh…yes ma'am." I replied.

"That's good." She nodded her head. "Can I hold something then?" She cut to the chase.

"How much you need?" I asked cautiously.

"How much you got?" She posed in a B-boy stance, arms crossed and feet spread apart.

"I only have about forty dollars in cash. The rest is all on my credit cards." I said honestly.

"Ok Jasmine, it was nice talking to ya." She dismissed me and got back into her car, letting the door slam and rolling her window up. *Well damn!*

Chapter Seven
Tionne

Standing out in the pouring rain, I hit the lock on the black Mercedes G-Wagon parked near the fountain in my driveway and hopped in. For a second, I just stared at my reflection in the rearview mirror. I looked like shit but I felt liberated. For the first time in a long time, I was free–no longer giving a fuck about image or what people thought about me. My mother used to tell me if a mofo wasn't paying my bills, then fuck 'em. I used to laugh then but now I was taking heed.

With no destination in mind, I hit the gate control in my whip and watched as the ten foot rod iron gates opened up. Instantly, a mob of photographers began snapping pictures.

"Where are you going Tionne?"

"Why don't you have on any clothing?"

"Where is Dallas?"

I didn't respond to a single question while revving the engine. Just as I prepared to pull off, my front door opened. I halfway expected Dallas to come chasing me down. However, I wasn't prepared for what I saw. This nigga was hurling my belongings out the front door piece by piece. At first, I tried to pay it no mind but the more my shit came flying out of the house, the more pissed off I got. "What are you doing!?" I yelled.

"I'm sick of your games, Tionne. You wanna leave then leave." Dallas said before tossing a box of Louboutins at me.

"So you're in the wrong but you mad because I'm leaving?" I jumped from the car completely oblivious to the paparazzi having a field day.

"Tionne, I give you everything and you still ain't happy. So fuck it, I'm done!" He barked.

"You're done? No nigga, I'm done!" Barging past him, I entered through the front door and opened the coat closet.

"What are you doing?" Now Dallas was behind me.

"I can show you better than I can tell you."

Bingo! I spotted a set of golf clubs he used at a charity event and pulled out the nine iron. "You want to damage my shit?" I laughed. "Ok, I got you."

"Girl, you better not do I what I think you gon' do?" Dallas's eyes were as big as saucers.

"You better get outta my way." I swung the club in his direction, intentionally avoiding his head.

With Dallas on my heels, I entered the kitchen and started busting out the glass windows on each cabinet. Next, I swung the golf club down and took to severely damaging the granite countertops. "What the fuck, Tionne!?"

"Move!" I screamed before taking my tyrant into the family room which was attached to the kitchen. Aligning the walls were several awards and trophies from the Grammys and VMAs.

"Don't do it!" Dallas yelled just before I resumed my crusade. CRASH! BANG! BOOM! Things went flying in every direction. After I cleared the wall, Dallas once again tried to stop me but he was no match for my speed. I ducked under his arm and headed into his office. "Tionne, you better cut this shit out right now!" Dallas ran up behind me.

With the laugh of a crazy woman, I raised the club above my head then swung it with all my might. It was with immense gratification that I watched Dallas's first framed platinum album shatter into pieces. "Are you fucking crazy!?" Endeavoring to salvage his most prized possession, Dallas pushed past me.

I don't know why but out of nowhere I started crying. "Dallas, why can't you just be right? Don't you know how much I love you? Don't you know how much I've given to this relationship?" I whimpered. "I love you more than I love myself sometimes. Why can't you just do right by me?"

"Tionne, I do love you and I want to be right baby; I do but..." Dallas took a seat in his desk chair then lowered his head in shame.

"Am I not good enough?" I continued to tear up. For years, the question stayed etched in my mind but I dared not ask it for fear of the answer.

"Tionne, you are good enough. I'm just too stupid to realize it at times." Dallas stood and came over to embrace me. "I'm a flawed man who has made my fair share of mistakes, but if you can give me one more chance, I swear on my father's grave, I'll try to do better."

"Dallas, do you know how many chances you've been given?" I pushed away from him. "I love you but I'm leaving."

"Please don't leave me." Dallas recognized that this time I was serious; I could tell he was scared to death.

"You and I both know this ain't working, so let's stop pretending." I'd come to this conclusion a long time ago but finally found the strength to act.

"Baby, I'll get my shit together. I don't want to lose you." Dallas was practically begging. Normally, I would find this amusing but today I was over it.

"I'm tired of being lied to and cheated on. I know you're tired of cheating and getting caught, so let's make it easy on both of us." I sighed before turning toward the door.

"Tionne, I can't live without you ma."

"At one time, I thought that was true Dallas but you'll survive; trust me." Smiling, I exited the room then made my way to the front door which was still wide-open.

"Are you leaving for a few days or filing for a divorce?" Dallas sounded like a saddened child.

"I'm gone." For the second time that night, I raised my right hand and chucked him the deuces. "It's time to do me."

"Baby please, think about giving us another try."

"The straw that broke the camel's back was the call I received the other day from the gynecologist." I turned to face him. "You gave me Chlamydia."

"What?" Dallas looked dumbfounded.

"That's right nigga; you don't even love me enough to use a rubber." Without another word, I kept on walking.

On the way out, I spotted a red Cavalli one piece lying on the floor and slipped it on. Dallas was still behind me; however, he remained quiet. Until now, I had never made good on my threats to leave; he was shocked but I wasn't. I had reached my breaking point. Therefore, I was done with a capital D. A bitch felt like Angela Basset in the movie *Waiting to Exhale* when she lit the car on fire.

As I walked away, my adrenaline level was rising. Yet, I was as cool as a cucumber when I stepped outside my house. The paparazzi were still there snapping pictures, fetching for a story but I didn't care. After hopping behind the wheel of the waiting G-Wagon, I put the pedal to the medal then sped off into my new life. "Fuck 'Love and Hip Hop'!"

Chapter Eight

Jasmine

"I mean why we gotta go all the way out to Somerset Mall?" Tracey whined from the backseat.

"Because Jasmine is the one paying for my shit and that's where she wants to go." Stacey tried to shut her sister down but Tracey wasn't having it.

"Fuck that! It's my birthday. The bitch ain't buying my shit and I want to go somewhere else." She pouted like a child.

"Take me home before I have to fuck your sister up." I demanded. I didn't know what her deal was. Ever since King got signed and we moved out the hood, Tracey and I have had beef. It was like she was mad that we made it.

"I ain't taking nobody home." She said to me. "T, you're right, it's your birthday, where do you wanna go?" She sided with her sister. I looked at her and rolled my eyes. Wherever it was, I just hoped this hood bitch picked a descent spot. I wanted to do my friend proper for her birthday and I couldn't do that at some flea market type shit.

"Let's roll to Uniquely Different. It's a new spot in Oak Park and it's all that." Tracey gushed. I'd been there before. She was right, the place was poppin' but I had to wonder how she could even afford to shop there. I was aware that she dated a few dope boys from time to time but no one consistent and I seriously doubted some nigga just looking for a booty call was footing the bill. Hopefully, she wouldn't try to steal anything because I was not going to bail her ass out.

We walked in the establishment like three women on a mission. "Hello. Welcome to Uniquely Different. I'm Diane, what can I help you with today?" A tall, red head, middle-aged, white woman with a short razor cut bob asked.

"It's my best friend's birthday. I want her to look fabulous at her party tonight and price is no object. What's new in your collection?" I asked while Tracey walked off to do her own thing. "I have a custom Gianni Santana piece that was just flown in yesterday." Diane said with a huge grin on her face. Pulling us toward the back showroom, she grabbed a few catalogs, showed us a few pieces then left us alone to try some things on.

"Do you see this place?" Stacey asked from her dressing room.

"Yes, this is top of the line." I added. The boutique was to die for, starting with the crystal chandeliers, hot pink and silver chic wall paper, ending with the black, lacquer fixtures, and grey, plush carpet.

"Let me see you?" I called out to my girl.

"I'm about to kill 'em softly with this one." Stace emerged from the dressing room wearing a royal blue, skin tight, mini dress. The neckline plunged and the back was barely there. It was *that* dress and in it, she was *that* bitch!

"Oh Stace, I'm loving it boo. I have some blue, suede Christian Louboutins that would go perfect with that dress."

"This dress is fifteen hundred dollars." Stace peeked a look at the price tag.

"It's all good. You know you're worth every

dollar." I smiled. "I'm going to find something for you to wear tomorrow at your party. It's going to be a surprise and you can't open it until then, okay." She nodded then I walked away to find my gift.

As I looked around the store, I noticed Tracey carry three dresses and a box of shoes to the register. I tried not to be too nosey but it was what it was, so fuck it.

"Your total today comes up to $6,280.17. Will you be paying with cash or credit?" The cashier asked. I was outdone and about to pass the hell out. *How in the hell was this girl getting her money?*

"Credit." She said, blowing me away. Cash was one thing but to have a credit card with that much on it was shocking for her. Somebody was keeping this bitch; I wondered who it was.

I went on about my business of browsing and finally stumbled across a red, satin dress with one strap and a pleated bottom. This was the one, so I went to the register to pay for it. My total for the two dresses and accessories that Stacey had picked

out was only $4,090.52. I handed the woman my
card and waited for my receipt.

"You didn't get nothing for yourself miss
high and mighty?" Tracey asked from behind me.

"Nope, today is all about my girl." I brushed
her off. This chick was not about to take me out of
character in this fine establishment.

"Is that so?" She raised an arched eyebrow.
"Or you just can't afford to?" Tracey added on the
sly.

"First of all hood rat, I don't need nothing
right now because my man just sent me on a
shopping spree in Italy last month. Second of all,
don't act like you be balling on the regular because
you just spent six G's. Lastly, don't fuck around and
get your ass beat on your birthday!" I said squaring
up to her. The bitch had me by several inches but I
wasn't about to back down. She wanted to go there,
so I served it up proper. With everything on my
mind, I would've whooped her ass in an instant
before God could even get the news.

"You think you the only one that can have a

baby and get a payday?" She said.

"I never looked at it like that, but yeah I guess I am." I smiled. "Your dusty ass has two babies and still no payday! Is that why you're salty? As a matter of fact, where in the hell are your baby daddies anyway?" I got her with that one.

"My kid's daddy," she put emphasis on the fact that both her kids shared the same father. "Is minding his fucking paper!"

"Is that so?"

"You think you're all that and something special, don't you." Looking me over from top to bottom, Tracey paid close attention to the three thousand dollar hair on my head, my frosted ears, neck, and wrist. The bitch almost gagged when her eyes landed on my 10 carat, princess cut, chocolate stone. "I want you to know that I could've had KJ if I wanted him, but I didn't," was her comeback.

"Then explain why I'm the one with the ring?" I extended my hand for good measure. She rolled her eyes and walked out of the store.

The rest of the evening went smoothly.

Tracey stayed in her lane and I stayed in mine. Besides, I was only there to ensure my bestie was having a ball. By the looks of it, she was partying like a rock star. I had bottle after bottle of Moet Rose sent over to the table. I wasn't drinking but it was my girl's favorite drink and I didn't want her to go empty. I danced on a few songs, wished my girl a happy birthday, and was out before they rolled in the cake. I needed to beat King home; by the time on my watch, I was pushing it. I had a little over an hour to get from downtown to the suburbs, shower, and get changed.

With no time to waste, my ass was whipping my black Lincoln Navigator onto I-75. Dodging in and out of traffic, I finally pulled up to my gate. "Shit!" I said aloud when I noticed King waiting for me on the walkway. Glancing down at the time, it read 11:15 p.m., which was thirty minutes away from the time King was due to arrive home. I had gotten a text from him hours ago confirming his expected arrival. I guess the plane had either landed early or he was lying about the time to catch me slippin'. "Hey baby." I stepped from the SUV cautiously.

"Where you been?" He mugged me.

"Oh, I forgot it was Stacey and Tracey's birthday party tonight. You know that's my best friend, so I couldn't miss it." I leaned in for a kiss but he turned away.

"Where did I ask you to be?" His jaw muscles tightened.

"Baby, you said you'd be back here just before midnight. I figured I could go to the party, stay for an hour or two, leave, and be home when you got here." I shrugged my shoulders. "I just wanted to make everybody happy."

"Fuck makin' everybody happy! I'm your man, your number one priority." He pointed at himself.

"King, I'm sorry." I tried to apologize.

"Yes, you are Jasmine. You are one sorry muthafucka." He turned then walked toward the house.

Watching him walk away, I stood there in

shock. On one hand, I couldn't believe King was acting like this. Then again, I could. This wasn't my first time being disrespected by him. As a matter of fact, it's been happening so frequently that I was rarely surprised whenever it happened anymore. I didn't feel like chasing after him so I sat on the stone staircase, removed my heels, sat them to the side, and put my head down in my lap. My life was going nowhere fast and I needed to do something quick. "Hey there baby girl," I heard my mother say from behind me.

"Hey mama, thanks for watching Jordan for me." I slid over as she sat beside me.

"That's my grandbaby; thank you isn't needed." She put her arms around me. "Are you okay?"

"I'm good mama. I just hate the way he treats me sometimes. It's like I can't do anything right. He makes me feel so worthless at times." I exhaled as she rubbed my back.

"Baby, a man will only treat you the way you allow him to. I see a lot of things around here I don't like but it's not my place to say anything. You're his wife and you signed up for this. Nobody can tell you what to do in your marriage it's up to you. You have to decide when you've had enough, baby girl. Mama can't hold your hand through everything."

She kissed my forehead. I loved my mother to death and was her spitting image. To this day, we're mistaken for sisters. Minus a few wrinkles, give or take a few pounds, my mama could still hang with the best of them. She put her life on hold to help me care for Jordan; I appreciated her so much. Without her support, I don't know what I would have done during the rough nights when my son cried for hours. She was there during his many doctor appointments and hospital stays, always reassuring me that everything would be okay.

"So you gon' stay out there all night?" King's voice boomed from the patio of our second floor master suite. I looked at my mama then she squeezed me tightly before standing to leave.

"Thanks mama, I love you." I said and

watched her until she was safely inside her 2014 Chevy Camaro.

After checking in on Jordan and finding him asleep in his hospital bed, I walked next door into our bedroom. "Damn, 'bout time you came in the house." King was lying across the triple king sized bed in nothing but Polo boxers.

"What's up baby?" I crawled across the bed and snuggled up next to him. "How was your flight?"

"It was cool. I'm just glad to be home lying in this bed next to you." He nibbled on my neck.

"I'm glad you're home too, baby. We missed you." I said seductively.

"What did you miss most about me?" His erect, eight inches of man-candy popped up suddenly. Kings soldier wanted some attention and I knew exactly what to do. Without saying a word, I slid down to the bottom of the bed and went to work.

"Damn baby," my man moaned which turned me on. "Suck that shit Jazzy, just like that baby."

"You like this baby?" I licked around the head of his penis.

"You know I do. Stop talking and keep sucking." He pushed my head down further until I began to gag.

"King, baby I can't go that deep." My eyes watered up and I began to cough.

"Baby, you better get your skull game up before I find a replacement." He joked.

"Whatever! I ain't going nowhere; me and you will be together forever." I got up from the bed and walked toward the spa-like bathroom.

"With head like that, you'd be lucky if I'm here when you come back from the bathroom." He grabbed the remote and turned on the television. Removing my dress, I tossed it at him playfully.

Chapter Nine
Zuri

The next morning, I was greeted by the smell of breakfast as well as the sound of running bath water. Part of Jason's ritual was to provide me with ladies-in-waiting, gifts, and a personal masseuse the day after he roughed me up. There were a total of three women contracted to run my bath, cook, and pamper me. I didn't have to lift a finger if I didn't want to. "Mrs. Armstrong, your bath awaits you." Karen, one of the ladies-in-waiting spoke from the doorway.

"I'll be there in a second." I replied with a groan. My body felt like shit and I'm certain it looked the same. I didn't have to see the bruises near my stomach to know they were there.

"I took the liberty of adding in your favorite lavender scent." Karen declared with a smile.

"Thank you." I stated before standing my nude self up from the bed and heading toward the four hundred square foot master en suite equipped with a vanity area, four head shower, and two person steam room.

"Hopefully, the water is to your liking."

"It's perfect." I replied after dipping my finger into the oversized, oval tub sitting in the center of the floor.

With Karen's assistance, I stepped into the tub and practically melted into the warm water. Bubbles were filled to the brim just the way I liked it. "I'll leave you to rest, Mrs. Armstrong, but I'm just outside the door if you need me." With a bow, Karen backed out of the bathroom and left me to my thoughts. Slowly, I lifted my head toward the mirror on the ceiling to assess the damage done to my body. As suspected, Jason's handprint was still slightly visible around my neck and my face was swollen. However, it wasn't too bad, nothing a little makeup wouldn't conceal.

"Thank God!" I mumbled to myself before leaning back into the bathtub. Things could've been much worse. I was thankful it wasn't. I remember one time Jason had broken my nose and dislocated my shoulder. That was, by far, the worse beatdown I had received at the hands of my husband.

"Zuri." I heard Syl before she entered the bathroom. "What the hell is going on around here? Who are all of these people?" The look on her face was pure confusion.

"It's your son's way of apologizing." I replied before closing my eyes, laying my head back then slipping down further into the tub. The water practically covered my ears.

"Fuck that! He needs to be taking his sorry ass to anger management!" She yelled.

"It doesn't happen that often." I conveyed with my eyes still closed. However, I could imagine Syl pacing back and forth in need of a cigarette, although she had quit almost two years ago.

"One time is too many Zuri. What in the fuck is wrong with you?"

"Let it go." I was trying my best to remain polite. I knew she was only trying to help me but it was what it was. If I had learned to accept it, she should too.

"What about Jelly?" Syl asked. My eyes popped open with the quickness. Her question caught me off guard.

"What about her?"

"Is this the kind of example you want to set for your daughter? Believe it or not, you're telling her it's okay to let a man put his hands on you as long as his pockets are deep."

"Sylvia, Jelly has nothing to do with my choices. As long as she is well-fed and taken care of, it shouldn't matter what's going on in my personal life." Unintentionally, my voice had raised an octave but I was furious with my mother-in-law for mentioning my daughter.

"Right now, Jelly is a baby, totally oblivious to the goings-on around here. Eventually, she'll grow up. What do you think will happen when she begins to see the violence for herself? What do you think will happen when she's the one picking you up off the floor time and time again?"

I didn't respond so Syl continued.

"Jelly is going to go right out and find a man

just like her father! Oh, just forget it." Visibly upset, Syl smacked her lips and left the room. I was glad too because I was tired of talking. Deep down inside, I knew Syl was right but what could I do? My hands were tied.

"Are you ready for me to wash your back?" I nodded. Smiling, Karen reentered the bathroom holding all the things needed for my bath.

Twenty minutes later, I was in my bedroom standing before the massive walk-in closet with eight foot doors and its own security camera. Everything inside was name brand and considerably expensive. Some of the pieces were custom made, one of a kind. Some items I had only worn once or never worn at all. As my eyes scanned the room, I was immediately drawn in by a yellow ensemble with a feathery train. I was wearing it the night I walked in Roberto Cavalli's fashion show in Paris.

It was a big night for both me and Jason. His sports representation agency had just secured the next Kobe Bryant. We were on cloud nine until Jason's ex best friend Fifty Shades went on a rampage calling him out about not being smart enough to graduate from high school. It was a secret that Jason never wanted to get out. He was mortified at the betrayal of his boy but took it out on me.

After the show, we went back to the hotel to change for the after-party. One thing led to another and Jason began beating me like I had stolen something. As usual, I said nothing. Not because I didn't want to but because his massive hand covered my mouth. When the brutality was over, he grabbed my shoes and purse then tossed them at me. When my purse hit the floor, a pregnancy stick spilled out. Silently, Jason grabbed it and read the positive results. Immediately, he tried to apologize but it was too late. We both knew the damage had been done as we watched the blood flow from between my legs.

Lulu, my second lady in waiting called from the door, "Mrs. Armstrong, your food is waiting."

"Give me a second." I sniffled before grabbing an YSL sweat suit off the shelf before slamming the closet door.

On the way downstairs, I checked in on my daughter who was still asleep in her pink princess toddler bed. Looking down at her precious face caused tears to pour down my face for two reasons. The first being I was so grateful I hadn't endured any violence while I carried her because I would've lost her too. The second reason was due to what Syl expressed. The thought of someone putting their hands on my baby girl nearly drove me crazy. They say history repeats itself; I would never want Jelly to be a man's punching bag. "Mrs. Armstrong, your breakfast is getting cold." Lulu popped her head in the door.

"I'm coming." I dabbed the corner of my eyes then headed for the kitchen.

As soon as I descended the spiral staircase, I noticed several boxes lining the edge of each stair– twenty in total. They were arranged from smallest to largest and were all wrapped in Tiffany blue wrapping paper. "Someone must love you very much!" Lulu commented while stopping to hand me the first box.

"I guess." I replied while tearing into the gift. It was a pair of sapphire earrings trimmed with diamonds. The second box was the matching necklace, the third a matching ring, and the fourth was of course, the matching bracelet. The next set of boxes contained clothing, shoes, and purses. Toward the end of the staircase, I unwrapped two boxes with Mink coats. The very last gift was the largest; it really had my attention. The boy had practically given me everything except another car.

"I wonder what it is?" Lulu was more excited than I was.

"I don't have a clue!" With a jolt of excitement, I bent down and shook the box. A few weeks ago, I mentioned getting a puppy; maybe this was it. However, nothing moved in the box and I didn't hear any noise coming from it. Quickly, I pulled the ribbon then tore into the paper with the nail of my index finger. Curiosity was killing both me and Lulu. Her eyes were as big as saucers.

"Oh my god!" I screamed. Resting inside the

box was several neat stacks of cash. Atop the large pile of money was an envelope. "This has to be at least sixty thousand dollars." I said to no one in particular.

"Open the letter." Lulu urged. Inside was a note which I read out loud.

"Zuri, grab a few friends and take them on a trip on me, all expenses paid. - Jay." Just like my husband not to even apologize. Sure the gesture was nice and the gifts were excellent but not once had he ever said he was sorry for hurting me.

"You're so lucky, Mrs. Armstrong." Lulu shook her head in admiration. I wanted to tell her that luck had nothing to do with this. I had earned every fucking thing he gave me plus more. Nevertheless, I smiled as I always did and remained silent.

Chapter Ten

Lyric

"Good luck today, baby." I yelled out of the window at Damien before I pulled out of the driveway. Today was his big audition; I was praying like hell things went well. We needed it. "Mom, can we order a pizza tonight?" Jonah asked from the backseat.

"We ain't got no money for a pizza." Leslie replied before I could say anything.

"Are we poor mommy? Leslie said we're poor." Jonah's words almost made me choke.

"Leslie, why would you say that?" I looked at my daughter with a puckered brow.

"That's what I saw online." Leslie replied with a whisper.

"Didn't I tell you about reading and believing everything off the Internet?"

"Yeah, but my friends are always showing me stuff. They said we're poor and daddy is a drug addict."

"Fuck your friends!" I spat before I knew it. Immediately, the car was silent. "Look, I'm sorry. I didn't mean to say that." Sighing, I decided that it was time to have a heart-to-heart with my children. As much as I wanted to shelter them from our situation I couldn't. "Listen guys, things have been tight for us, I'm not going to lie, but we are not poor."

"So why does the Internet blogs say it?" Leslie looked at me.

"Sometimes, the media has a way of bending the truth for public enjoyment. They put out lies and gossip about celebrity personas because it makes their company more popular."

"So why can't we just get online and tell them it's not true?" This time it was Jonah asking the questions.

"Baby, we can't fight them all so it's better to just leave it alone. Eventually, they will find someone else to pick on and our story will be old news." Although I was smiling, I wanted to cry so badly. It was one thing to talk about me and

Damien. I could handle that but when it started affecting my children, my feelings were on a whole other level. "Listen guys, I promise things will get better and this too shall pass okay. The money and the fame may come and go but as long as our family stays together that's all that matters, right?"

"Yes ma'am." They replied in unison just as we pulled up to their school. This had been the longest ten minute ride to school ever. "You guys have a good day and I'll pick up two pizzas tonight, okay Jonah."

"Cool. Thanks mom." Jonah gave me a kiss on the cheek.

"Bye mom." Leslie smiled before jumping out the car. I watched until my kids were in the building before releasing the brake. Just as I did, Mrs. Clementine, the head of the school, flagged me down.

"Fuck." I snarled under my breath.

"Mrs. Robertson, did Leslie tell you that without her tuition she won't be able to partake in today's field trip?"

"Her tuition is in her book bag. Sorry I forgot." I tried to pull off again.

"Did you send Jonah's as well?" Mrs. Clementine continued.

"No, actually I didn't. I'll send his next week."

"Mrs. Robertson, let me remind you that our waiting list is very long. When you enrolled your children, you were made aware that their tuition was due no later than the end of first semester. We're nearing the end of third semester. If you don't have it, please don't hold up spaces for children with funds."

I couldn't believe this bitch had the audacity to come at me the way she did. The newly refined Lyric would've nodded my understanding then pulled off. However, the old B-More Lyric was the one behind the wheel today. If this lady wanted to start shit, I was about to serve it proper. Putting the car in park, I opened the door and stepped out.

"Look Valerie," I said addressing her by her first name. "I don't know who the fuck you think you are to be coming at me sideways but let me inform you that I'm not the one to be talked to like a child!" I snapped. "So what, I missed the due date on the fucking tuition. My children have been coming here for years and this is the first time it has happened. Second of all, you're failing to remember all of the money my husband and I have donated to this got damn school. Third of all, if you ever–and I do mean ever–talk slick and address me in that manner again, I will not hesitate to whoop your ass!" I was on ten, totally oblivious to the crowd of parents and paparazzi watching and recording the scene word for word.

"Well I see you can take the girl out of the ghetto but you can't take the ghetto out of the girl." Valerie replied.

"Oh I'm gonna show you ghetto." I warned.

"You lay one hand on me and I won't hesitate to expel your children and sue you for whatever you have left." She readjusted the jacket on her too tight gray suit then turned on the balls of her kitten heels and retreated toward the safety of the school.

"Care to comment on what just happened, Lyric?" One of the reporters stuck his camera in my face. In a fit of rage, I didn't hesitate to swing at him. He dodged me; I was glad he did. Had I hit him or damaged his camera, I would've paid dearly. It was time to get the fuck out of here.

"Move!" I screamed while pushing past the nosey bystanders. Hopping back inside of my car, I put the pedal to the medal then sped off.

After riding twenty minutes in silence to my appointment, the bluetooth in my car rang. The caller ID read my mother's name. At first, I started not to pick up but decided against it. "Hello mother."

"Hey pooh." She sounded as if life was perfect; I guess it was for her when she didn't have a care in the world. Everything she owned, I was footing the bill for.

"What's up?"

"I was calling because your father and I are celebrating fifty years in two months and I thought it would be great to have a little party to celebrate."

"Mom, I really…"

"I was thinking maybe you could rent out the ballroom at the country club and we could invite at least fifty of our closest friends and church members." She rambled as if this had been planned for months.

"Mom, I just…

"That number doesn't include family, so it'll be approximately two hundred. My favorite color is cream and your father's is brown. Maybe that could be the theme." She continued without pause. "I took the liberty of calling Changa and we set up a meeting for this Friday." Changa was an event specialist I used from time to time and he was quite pricey.

"How are you paying for this?" I asked, realizing that would quiet her down.

"Huh?" She asked, obviously dumbfounded.

"I'm on a budget and I can't afford to throw you and daddy a lavish party right now." Even though this was the first time I was telling my mother no, I knew she wouldn't like it.

"I never ask you for anything and the one time I do you turn me down?" She sounded outdone. I wanted to remind her that while she hadn't asked me for anything it didn't stop me from paying her mortgage, buying her and my fathers car, sending them a monthly allowance as well as sending them on lavish vacations twice a year.

"Mom, we're going through some financial issues right now. If something changes, I will cover the party, if not, I just can't."

"Um Hm." My mother said before smacking her lips. Her reaction was a little hurtful. A mother should've been more caring and understanding. She should've asked me if there was anything she could do instead of being selfish. Sadly, I learned a long time ago that money changed people for the worse. The minute Damien hit it big, I began to hear from people I hadn't spoken to in years. Family members began to call with all kind of sob stories and friends started changing.

"Look mom, I have to go. I'll call you later."

I ended the call and pulled over to the side of the road. The tears in my eyes had taken over and I could no longer see. Silently, I sobbed until I had nothing left. I was tired of everything and everybody. I just needed some me-time before I went crazy but that wasn't going to happen anytime soon.

Seconds after getting myself together, I pulled up and pressed the call button on my client's gate opener. "Come on in Lyric." Ken replied and buzzed me in. He had been my client ever since he joined the NBA. I normally supplied him with suits for press conferences or streetwear but today he had put in a request for women's clothing.

After grabbing my garment bags from the rear of my whip, I headed up to Ken's condominium. He was standing in the doorway wearing a small, white tee, brown, man Capri pants, and a pair of canvas gym shoes. "There's my girl with the goods." He stepped aside and permitted me to enter.

"What's up homey?" I reached for a super

high-five after placing my things down.

"What you got for me, Mrs. L?"

"First of all, you haven't even told me who I was shopping for, what her style was or anything. All you said was size eight and I'm supposed to work with that?" I laughed. Ken was one of my favorite clients. His personality was amazing and he was always a pleasure to work with.

"I knew you would make it work so I ain't worried." Ken took a seat on the white thinking chair in his living room.

"At least tell me if she's someone special." I said while pulling the clothing from the bags and laying them out on the sofa.

"Her name is Diamond and she's very special." He was smiling that contagious smile of his. "I think she's the one but I have to run her pass mom dukes first, ya feel me."

"Oh lord, this must be serious then." In all the time Ken had been my client, I never saw him with a woman or even mention one for that matter. His head was so far into the game of basketball, people began speculating about his sexual preference.

"It is and I need everything to go right which is why I called you." Ken laughed. "I need baby girl to trade in those booty shorts for a nice sundress."

"Don't tell me she's a hot mama, Ken. Mama Tucker ain't gone play that." I looked back at him while pulling out the shoes and accessories. I'd heard his mother was a beast and his sister was very protective of her little brother.

"Diamond has a little edge about her, which I love, but I don't want her to be misjudged by my family because of her attire." Ken looked down at the floor.

"How do you think Diamond will feel when she finds out you're trying to change her though?"

"I'm not trying to change her for good just for the weekend." He laughed.

"I'm just saying, love shouldn't come with limits. Your love life is none of my business but if you love Diamond, you should love her flaws and all. What if she tried to change your wardrobe or told you to talk a certain way before you met her family. Would you like that?" I looked at Ken like a little brother. I didn't want him to lose someone that obviously made him happy for the sake of pleasing his mama.

"Damn Lyric, now you got me feeling bad." Ken sat back in the seat while pondering my words.

"I'm not trying to do that but you know I keep it one hundred; beating around the bush ain't my thing." I shrugged with a smile.

"Speaking of which," Ken cleared his throat. "Don't get mad at me for asking but I saw an article about your company being in the red. Is that true, Lyric?"

Instantly, the air in the room became quite thick. I was mortified to have a client asking me about my financial report. My first reaction was to lie. "Of course not."

"Lyric." Ken eyed me suspiciously. "Come on man. I thought me and you were better than that."

"Fine." I smacked my lips. "Yes, my company is in the red. If things don't turn around soon, I will have to close the doors to my business. It's nothing to be alarmed about right now that's why I didn't say anything but since you asked..." I felt defeated. For a very long time, I was able to keep my business personal from my friends, family, and clients. If Ken had read the article, there was no telling who else knew I was two steps away from the poverty line.

"Damn Lyric, I was hoping that shit wasn't true!" He sat back up in his seat. "What you gon' do?

"I wish it wasn't Ken." I sighed. "Life happens but I'll do everything I can to keep my doors open." I replied honestly.

"How much, Lyric?"

"I'm not here for a handout, Ken. Now that you know what I'm facing, I want you to obtain a backup stylist just in case." After setting up the clothing, I turned to face him.

"Look, I only want to work with you. We've

been rocking since day one." He stood from his chair. "How much is your yearly retainer?"

"I charge forty thousand a year." Usually, stylist had two options when taking on clients. The first was to be paid per event. The second option was to be paid in advance for the entire year. Basically, it meant you were on call for every affair your client attended at a discounted rate. Up until now, Ken was only a pay per event client.

"I got you."

"Ken, you don't have to do this." I didn't want him to see me as unprofessional for divulging my personal business as a way of swindling his money.

"Stop it." He walked away briefly before coming back with a check. "You're like family, Lyric. I'll never see your business in the red as long as I can help."

"This check is for eighty thousand dollars!" My hand was trembling. "Ken," was all I could say before tears filled my eyes. I was totally overwhelmed by his kindness. "This is too much."

"That's for me and Diamond." Ken smiled. "I want you to style us both. She's going to be my wife real soon and I gotta make sure she's flawless at all times."

"Thank you so much. You really have no idea what this means." I was practically balling like a baby. This boy had no idea that he had just paid my kids' tuition, put food in my refrigerator, and saved me from the repo man.

"Lyric, I know you're a good person with a great heart. In life, sometimes, we encounter storms; but that doesn't mean God isn't still in the blessing business." Ken wrapped his arms around me, hugging me tightly. I knew I was a mess and wanted badly to pull myself together. However, right now, I couldn't let go of my seven foot savior. My ass was practically shouting about the blessing I'd just received as well as the word Ken had just delivered. It was confirmation that God was real and He would never see the righteous forsaken, even when we thought He was too busy to hear our cries.

Just then, the front door opened. In walked

the infamous Diamond, looking like she was ready to throw punches.

Chapter Eleven
Diamond

"What the fuck is really going on around this bitch?" I asked my man and the little bitch he was all hugged up on.

"Diamond, this is my stylist Lyric. I had her bring some pieces over for you." Ken replied nervously.

"Nigga, I'm grown as hell; I can pick out my own shit!" Prepared for war, I sat my purse down on the table. "Where I come from, bitches get killed for shit like this!"

"Diamond, I don't want your man." Homegirl sniffled and wiped her eyes. "I'm married to Damien Roberts." The skank said it like he was someone special.

"The crackhead?" I replied without remorse.

"Diamond!" Ken snapped. The bulging vein in his forehead indicated I had gone too far.

"Fuck you bitch!" Shorty popped back at me before turning to my man. "Ken, I don't have to take this shit. Here's your money; I'm out."

"Lyric, don't go." Ken grabbed her arm. I didn't like the gesture but I knew enough to keep my mouth closed. "Diamond, what the hell is wrong with you? This lady is a good friend of mine who came to do me a favor and this is how you act."

"Baby, I'm sorry." I didn't like being in the doghouse with my man so I tried to change my tune.

"Don't apologize to me, apologize to Lyric." He scolded me like a child.

"I'm sorry, Lyric. I don't mean any harm; I'm just territorial about mine." I said begrudgingly. "Think about it, I walk in and see a woman all hugged up with my man and my mind went off the deep end." Casually, I walked over and wrapped my arms around my boo, creating distance between the two of them.

"I understand. It's all good." Lyric nodded. I'm sure she knew exactly where I was coming from. "I can assure you, there is nothing going on this way. Ken just retained me to style you for the year, so I hugged him to thank him for the business that's all." Lyric smiled.

"Baby, you did?" I turned to Ken.

"I gotta have my wifey looking her best at all times." Ken replied.

"Well alright then." I turned back to Lyric. "Let me see what you picked out for his wifey." I walked over to the pieces laid out on the sofa.

"Well I was only able to pull a few pieces because Ken called me last minute. He didn't give me much to work with other than your size. I hope you like it. If not, let's go back to the drawing board."

"Girl, this shit is deadly!" I squealed after looking over the ensembles Lyric had chosen without knowing me from a can of paint. "These Louboutins ain't even hit the runway yet."

"I have some good connections." Lyric said then walked over to the clothes and started holding them up to my body. It felt good to be made a fuss over. I loved being the girlfriend of a wealthy nigga.

"Lyric is good people Diamond. I want y'all

to hangout from time to time. She could really show you the ins and outs of being a celebrity wife."

"Wife?" I was smiling so damn hard that all my teeth, cavities, and tonsils were showing.

"I would be happy to show her the ropes." Lyric nodded. "I think Diamond would make a great NBA wife."

"I love the sound of that!" I squealed. "Uh baby, don't you have a game to be getting to?" I looked up at Ken who backed away with his hands up.

"I get the picture. I'll leave you guys to it."

"See you." Lyric and I said in unison.

"Can you hook me up for the game tonight? I need to be fly."

"Absolutely, this is what I do!" Lyric said before going to work on my outfit for the night.

When it was all said and done, homegirl had laced me with a black, v-neck top with ruffles at the bottom and a denim, pencil skirt and accessories. I felt sexy yet sophisticated. "You'll fit right in with those basketball wives tonight!" Lyric snapped her finger.

"Thank you Lyric and again, I'm sorry for coming at you like that." I was remorseful because I had totally misjudged her. She was a really cool person.

"No thank you needed boo. Call me anytime you need something and I got you." She began packing up her belongings.

"Ken is planning to have a get together with his family sometime soon. Do you think we could meet up and go shopping before that, so I can impress his mother?"

"Of course, Diamond." Lyric smiled.

"I really like him and I know what his mother thinks about me will determine if I get the green light or not." As I spoke, I surprised myself with how open I was being with this stranger. However, Lyric was really down-to-earth and we had a connection.

"Diamond, if I may drop some jewels on you, it would be to always remain yourself. I understand that you want to impress his mother, but don't change so much that you lose yourself in the process." With a smile, Lyric swung two garment bags across her shoulder and headed for the door. I wanted to tell her there was so much dirt on my résumé that it wouldn't be a bad idea to lose my old self completely. I would've changed my whole identity if I could just to escape my ratchet past. Had I known my path would lead me to this castle, living with my prince, I would've never kissed all those frogs in the first place.

Two hours later, I had shit, showered, and shaved. Right as I slid the towel dress over my head, the buzzer buzzed. Knowing it was my girl, Nisha, who was accompanying me to the game tonight, I buzzed her in without question. Seconds later, I heard the knock on the door and ran downstairs to unlock it. Because of the security gate and surveillance camera surrounding the condo, there was no peep hole in the door. Therefore, I swung it wide open without a second thought. Standing there was Satan himself, dressed in a red Dickie outfit and a St. Louis snapback with a toothpick dangling from between his lips. "Duck!" I gasped, nearly jumping from my skin.

"A nigga had to come a long fucking way to find your ass." He smirked before stepping into the condo like he owned it.

"Why? How?" The words in my mind wouldn't form a proper sentence as I took in the ungodly sight before me.

Donald "Duck" Marshall was a skeleton I wish had stayed his ass in the fuckin' closet. Two years ago, he was my man and a big time dope boy in Missouri. Duck was getting money faster than I could spend it, which is why I stayed with his ugly ass and endured all the shit he subjected me to. After being hit with both distribution and possession charges, Duck was sentenced to twelve years. The time apart provided a window of opportunity for me to do what I do best, which was to rob his ass blind. I stole everything he owned–money, jewelry, clothing, furniture, and cars. Then I sold everything on the black market. Temporarily, my pockets were swollen but so was the lump in my throat the minute I got word that his ass had been set free sixty days later due to a "technicality." Using the last of my earnings from his shit, I hopped on the first plane to Los Angeles and never looked back. I thought being halfway across the world was far enough. However, by the looks of things, I should've gone a lot further.

"What are you doing here?" I tried to calm my nerves.

"Diamond, you're too young to have Alzheimer's." He chuckled while checking out the condo. I watched his eyes gaze over the expensive paintings on the wall and my stomach turned. "You know exactly why I'm here."

"Look Duck, I'm sorry about what happened back then. I was young and stupid." I followed behind him.

"Sorry? Oh, you will be sorry if I don't get my bread." He stopped abruptly, causing me to run into his back. Prison had done wonders for his body. The shit felt like a brick wall.

"I don't have any money." I pleaded.

"You must think I'm stupid." Duck turned to face me. "Bitch, I know whose house this is! You're fuckin' a millionaire; so getting my bread shouldn't be that hard." Duck waltzed over to the sofa and flopped down, putting his dirty shoes on the white furniture.

"Duck, me and him ain't like that. I mean I can get a little dough but not that much." I tried to calm my shaky hand.

"Diamond, I don't give a fuck if you have to rob this nigga like you did me or sell that stank ass pussy." His stone cold grimace had me shook. "I'll give you two weeks to put two mill in my hand before you come up missing."

"Two million!?" I almost fell over.

"Two million dollars in two weeks or I will put two bullets right between your got damn eyes." Duck made his fingers imitate a gun then pulled the trigger.

118

Chapter Twelve
Tionne

The sound of the ringing phone on the nightstand stirred me from my slumber. "Hello."

"Mrs. Foster, this is the front desk. Sorry to disturb you but there is a problem with your credit card." The man on the other end cleared his throat.

"What kind of problem could there be with a black card?" I snapped. "It's limitless, so there shouldn't be anything wrong with it."

"Actually, it was declined ma'am."

"Declined?" I sat up in the plush king sized bed. "What?"

"It declined. I'm sorry."

"There has to be some mistake!" I jumped from the bed as if it were on fire. "Try this one." I fumbled for my purse and retrieved an AMEX. After reciting the sixteen digit number, I waited.

"Unfortunately, this one declined as well."

"Are you for real?" I shook my head and grabbed another card. Once again, I relayed the number and once again, I was told the shit declined. Finally fed up with this nonsense, I just told the guy to give me a second and I would be down with cash. "Ain't this a bitch!" I snapped while slipping on my pants and a pair of shoes. Without calling the card companies, I knew Dallas had cut me off. Lucky for me, I had enough cash on hand to cover a few nights at the W as well as a personal credit card that I applied for on my own.

With much attitude, I stormed down the hallway, stepped on the elevator, and headed to the front desk. Waiting for me was a tall, white man with no facial hair. "Ah Mrs. Foster." He smiled with recognition.

"I'm sorry about the cards. It appears my husband is playing dirty." I reached into my pocket and handed over the money. While the guy went about ringing me up, I glanced above his head where the television was. It was on E. They were covering the story on Joan Rivers but the on the bottom of the screen, I saw my name. I had missed the beginning of the caption but the end read,

Tionne Foster was seen speeding away from the couple's Calabasas home in rage. Sources say the couple is headed for splitsville again!

"Thank you, ma'am. Here is your receipt."

"Thanks." I took the paper then headed back toward the elevator. In the lobby was a small convenience store. I stopped in to grab an orange and a pack of Tylenol to cure the headache that was assuredly lurking.

"Oh my god, is that her!?" I could hear from behind me.

"I think it is." Someone else replied. As I approached the counter, they approached me.

"Excuse me miss. Can you sign this please?" Some pimple-faced white girl with braces extended a tabloid my way. I looked down to see myself and Dallas on the cover with a squiggly line between us. Somehow, the owners of Sloppy Gossip, a popular tabloid magazine, had managed to get my story and print it in less than twenty-four hours.

"Little girl, you better get out of my face." Turning to face the counter, I tried to ignore the little bitch.

"I can see why Dallas is with a white woman instead of her." She giggled with her friend.

"I know right." The friend laughed. "Black women have bad attitudes."

"First of all..." I turned to reply but lucky for me, they had placed the magazine back on the rack and walked out.

"Don't let them get to you girl." The cashier shook her head before handing me my items in a bag along with my change.

"Thanks." I grabbed my shit and quickly retreated back to my room.

As soon as I entered, my cell phone started ringing. It was my girl Zuri. Although I wanted to talk to her, I let the call go to voicemail then quickly dialed my house. "Hello." Some unfamiliar sounding female answered while giggling.

"Who the fuck is this!?" I barked.

"Who the fuck do you want it to be?" She laughed.

"Bitch, give Dallas the phone." I was

beyond pissed off.

"Hello." Dallas answered as if it was perfectly normal to have another bitch in my house.

"Who the fuck was that and why the fuck is she there?"

"That was, Bridget, my new assistant."

"You fuckin' bastard! I haven't been gone long and you already have a new bitch living up in my house?" Although crying was the last thing on my mind, I couldn't stop the tears from forming. I tried to act tough but this shit was hurtful.

"Tionne, chill out with all of that. I ain't got nobody living here." Dallas laughed.

"You ain't shit but a dirty fuckin' dog, Dallas. One day you're gonna end up with flees!" I was seething.

"You can kill that noise alright. Besides T, you left me, remember? When you walked out the fucking door, you gave me permission to do me. Don't get mad now."

"Fuck you Dallas!"

"Tionne, is there a reason that you called in

the first place?" Dallas sighed. "I have shit to do."

"You cut off my cards?"

"Actually, they weren't your cards in the first place. But yeah I cut them off." The sound of Dallas's voice was sickening.

"Just last night, you said you couldn't live without me. Today, you're being mean and vindictive. Your bipolar ass needs to see a fuckin' doctor."

"Well I thought I couldn't live without you until you left. That's when I realized my house is still my house, my cars are still mine, my bills will be paid without you, and I'm still the fuckin' CEO of my own shit without you." Dallas started laughing hard. "You see Tionne, it's you that actually can't live without me. When you left here last night screaming that independent shit, you actually thought you was about that life so I figured I would play along. I cut off the cards, closed the joint account, and I'll be turning your cell phone off shortly. Later today, someone will come and pick up the G-wagon since I know you're at the W." He snickered. "Tionne, if you want to be independent so bad, I want you to see what those independent bitches go through. Life ain't always greener on the other side ma."

"You're a fucking asshole!"

"When you come to your senses, I'll be here waiting. Until then, remember to never bite the hand that feeds you."

Chapter Thirteen
Jasmine

Business ran as usual for the five days that King was home. The chef cooked, I cleaned the house, and spent most of my time with Jordan. King on the other hand, had a lot of running around to do. Sunday, he slept all day. Therefore, we didn't make it to Stacey's party. On Monday, he played basketball with some of his old friends from high school then hit the studio to record. Tuesday, he headed to one of the local after-school activity centers and talked with the kids. Wednesday was his busiest day because he took meetings with the label execs and reps from his clothing line to discuss the direction of his brand. Thursday was no fun either because he slept all day *again*. King barely acknowledged Jordan when he was home. It used to upset me. Unfortunately, over the past four years, I'd grown accustomed to it. Today was Friday and we were in Los Angeles for the early screening of Kings new movie, "Black In The Hood." I didn't know what the movie was about. Nonetheless, I was really excited to see it on the big screen. My man was a movie star now and I was very proud of him.

King was a bit antsy and on edge earlier at the hotel. He had snapped on the stylist and my makeup artist. For that reason, I stayed away from him until it was time to leave. I didn't need him being upset with me on such a beautiful day. As we rode down Hollywood Boulevard, I couldn't help but notice that King couldn't be still. He squirmed in his seat like a child that needed to use the potty. "It's okay baby. I know you did great!" Recognizing he was extremely nervous, I smiled reassuringly. We waited in line with the other fleet of vehicles for about twenty minutes. During the entire time, a man walked along side the SUV while speaking into a device on the cuff of his jacket.

"What is he doing?" I asked King.

"Oh, they do that so the camera crew and reporters can hear whose approaching. This shit is live on the air, so they need to be ready with questions." He explained as we finally made it to the front of the huge building. "King James in vehicle thirteen." The guy spoke into his cuff then opened the door.

When we stepped from the black Escalade, cameras and microphones were instantly placed in our faces. "So KJ, how does it feel to take a break from rapping and pursue an acting career?" A white reporter with a large nose asked.

"It feels awesome ya know. It's something I've always wanted to do, so I'm thankful I was given this opportunity." King flashed a smile and winked at the camera for good measure. He reached for my arm then we walked down the red carpet as more cameras flashed.

"KJ, what are you wearing tonight?" An Asian woman asked.

"This is Valentino." King opened his pinstriped suit jacket, did a slow spin then posed for a quick picture.

"Thank you KJ, enjoy the premier and congrats on the movie." The reporter said as we walked into the lobby of the Belle Grand hotel and

Theater. People were everywhere and I was excited. I had already spotted a few vets like Denzel and Angela. I tried to compose myself and not act like a groupie but it was tough.

"Baby, should we go to our seats? The premier starts in less than ten minutes." I glanced down at my Movado timepiece.

"Jasmine, do these people look like they're in a rush to you? Chill the fuck out!" He snapped.

"Damn King, I was just telling you so we won't miss anything." I said in my defense.

"Yeah, well don't tell me anything else tonight alright. The only thing I need you to do is look pretty and be quiet." He released my arm then walked toward the group of people that I recognized as the movie cast. I didn't know what to do, so I just stood there like a fool. I watched King smile for a few more pictures and drop a few more lines to reporters.

I scanned the room for a familiar face, but this scene was different from what I was accustomed to. At least at music industry events,

there was always a person I could talk to.
Sometimes, there were producers, DJs, or a few hip
hop wives. Other times, it was the singer or rapper
themselves. Either way, I was in my element and
felt at ease because I was in the "in" crowd. I could
speak the lingo and knew all about the latest drama
and gossip. This shit was too upscale; I felt out of
place, like a party crasher. The room was packed
with men in expensive suits and women in exquisite
gowns, draped up and dripping with millions of
dollars in jewelry. Soft music played in the
background as waiters distributed champagne flutes
and finger food. Small chatter and light laughter
flowed throughout the room. I couldn't help but
wonder how a person could feel so alone in a room
full of people.

Just as I was about to check my watch for
the third time, I noticed a fine gentleman staring at
me. "I'm sorry, am I in your way?" I asked since I
was standing in front of the doors to the theater. All
of the other people had walked around me.
Therefore, I thought this guy was just trying to give

me a hard time.

"No beautiful, you're not in my way. Actually," he pulled at his tie. "I was just coming over here to introduce myself. I'm Bradley Homes, and you are?" I almost wet myself when he extended a hand and hit me with his Rembrandt smile. Mr. Homes was fine to say the least. He stood at least 6 feet 7 inches with sun-kissed skin and short, dark, wavy hair. My guess was he was Hawaiian or something.

"Mr. Homes, my name is Jasmine, Jasmine James." I stuttered.

"Nice to me you, Jasmine." He smiled again. "I saw you come in with King James. Is he your date?"

"No, well yes, he's my husband." I needed to get it together and fast.

"Husband?" He sounded shocked. "I should've figured that since James is your last name too." He chuckled. "Anyway, I just wanted to come over and ask if you wouldn't mind passing him my card. I produce movies; and I have an upcoming role that I would love to cast him in, the guys a natural. I would've given him the card myself but I turned my back and he disappeared on me. The movie is scheduled for production in two months. Maybe we could do lunch before he leaves California and talk about it." He looked back at the crowd that was beginning to thin out and I did the same.

"Yes, of course Mr. Homes. I will definitely pass the card, along with your message to King; and lunch sounds great!" I reached for the card then placed it inside of my red sequined Chanel clutch.

"Thanks, Mrs. James. If you'll excuse me, I've got to get going. My wife is waiting for me; she's ready to take our seats." He patted my shoulder and I smiled.

Time was ticking; we were about to miss our premier. I had already seen most of the cast members go inside the theater. All except King and that damn Melissa Valentine. I was about to reach for my cell phone when out of nowhere, somebody snatched my wrist and yanked it. "Bitch, are you serious? So you just gon' disrespect me like that?"

It was King looking deranged.

"What?" I asked while Melissa Valentine stood there snickering. "What the fuck are you talking about King; and where in the hell have you been?" I wanted to know.

"Don't fucking question me? I'm the one who needs to be asking questions. Who the fuck was that Puerto Rican looking nigga you was over here flirting with?" He squeezed my wrist tighter.

"Flirting? Wasn't nobody over here flirting? He came over here to…" I was cut off by King's voice.

"Over here to do what bitch? I can't take your simple ass nowhere! All a nigga asked you to do was get dressed, look pretty, and shut the fuck up! You didn't need to start talking to nobody!" He barked.

"Excuse me sir, if you can't lower your voice, and calm down, we're going to have to ask you to leave. The guests inside the theater are beginning to complain." A security guard explained to King.

"I ain't going no fucking where bruh, so you need to back the hell up and let me handle my lady." King tried to brush the dude off but it wasn't happening.

"Look partner, I've warned you already. Next, I'm gonna have to call the police." The guard threatened.

"Well my dude, you do what you gotta do!" King shot back after letting my wrist go.

"King, calm down baby; we don't need the police here." I tried reaching for his hand; I was ready to say fuck the movie and leave.

"Bitch, get yo' hood rat ass away from me. I can't take you no damn where without you dick hoppin' over to the next nigga with money." He looked at me like he didn't even know who I was.

"Are you serious right now!?" I screamed. People had begun to exit the movie theater and gather around us like we were the damn premier.

"Yeah, you raggedy bitch! I made you and this is how you do me? Where that nigga at?" He started searching through the crowd; I was beyond embarrassed. Putting my head down in shame, I attempted to walk away as quickly as possible.

"Bitch you ain't going nowhere until I speak to that nigga. Where he at?" He pulled my hair and yanked me back.

"King stop it! You're hurting me; stop it please!" I begged while the crowd of faces looked on.

"Hey young brother don't treat that beautiful sister like that." Someone spoke out.

"Where is the nigga at, Jasmine?" He yanked again, causing me to trip on a snag in the carpet. One of my Jimmy Choos came off, causing me to hit the floor hard.

"King, stop it! Please, baby stop!" I cried as he drug my ass. I tried my darndest to hold my dress down. Even so, I'm sure my bare ass and shaved vagina was showing.

"Stop it? Am I embarrassing you Jasmine? Well you embarrassed me! You're my wife and you over here flirting with a nigga at my event. How am

I supposed to feel?" He stopped and looked down at me.

"King, the man came over to give me a business card." I said through tears. Since he was no longer dragging me, I quickly opened my clutch and produced the business card. "He wants you to take a role in his new movie. He couldn't find you, so he gave it to me." I stood and wobbled over to my other shoe. My entire body was in pain. All I wanted to do was bounce. My Indian weave was in disarray and flying all over the place. My sequined dress was ruined, the red, swollen rug burns on my thighs and arms looked hideous, my makeup was through, and I was mortified. Not only had King's tantrum been witnessed by a room full of influential people, it had also been recorded by the many cameras in the building.

"Ma'am, can I call somebody for you?" A young security guard asked as I walked away from the crowd.

"No, but is there a back way out of here?" I asked with tears.

Chapter Fourteen
Zuri

Beep. Beep. I leaned on the horn just as Tionne ran out into the rain. She had been waiting in the lobby of the hotel for me to pick her up and take her to her lawyer. She knew her car was safe in the hotel's parking garage and didn't want to run the risk of Dallas taking it if she left and had to park on the street.

"Thank you for coming to pick me up." Tionne reached over for a hug.

"Why the hell did I have to wait until you needed a ride for you to pick up the phone and call me?" I asked. "I thought we were tight." Tionne had been held up at the W for over a week now and I was annoyed that she hadn't answered my calls or dialed me sooner.

"Girl, you know it ain't like that. I just needed some time you know." Tionne sighed.

"Bitch, I got all the time in the world. I would've come over and cried with you, yelled with you, and kicked that muthafucka's door in if need be." My joke was to lighten the mood but Tionne merely stared out the window. "It's gonna be alright." I patted her thigh.

"Is it Z? I mean I just can't believe that bastard threatened to steal my fuckin' car. Who does that?"

"A lame ass nigga that's who." I laughed and this time Tionne did too. "Seriously, he calls himself breaking you down so you'll come crawling back but fuck him. I got you bitch!" I reached for a high five.

"I know you do Z." Tionne slapped her palm into mine and we shared a brief moment of silence.

She and I had been best friends going on ten years now. We met at a fashion show during fashion week in New York. Tionne had been invited as the guest of the designer and I of course, was one of the models. The show was such a success that the designer decided to treat a few of his models and friends to dinner and drinks. As luck would have it, Tionne was seated next to me. We hit it off instantly and have been trump tight ever since. In a world full of fake friends and false admirers, Tionne was my ace. There was nothing in the world I wouldn't do for her and vice versa.

"Thanks Z; I really owe you one." Tionne reclined in the seat.

"Girl, I know if the shoe was on the other foot you would have me too." I released the brake and put the SUV in motion.

"That's what friends are for although your ass has the perfect marriage and won't ever need me." She smiled, "Jason is the shit!"

"I guess." I shrugged. Tionne was my bestie but some things needed to remain between husband and wife.

"I wish Dallas was more like Jason–faithful, loving, giving, and finneeeee!" She exclaimed. I wanted to tell her to be careful what she wished for but instead, I concentrated on the road.

During the ride, no one said a word. Therefore, Tionne decided to break the silence. "Aren't you going to ask me why I left this time?"

"No I wasn't." I said without looking at her. This wasn't my first rodeo with Tionne and Dallas. I'm sure it wasn't my last. As a result, I learned long ago not to ask questions.

"Why not?"

"Because T, it doesn't matter." I sighed. "Look, don't take this the wrong way but I know the way this is going to play out already. This is not the first time you've called me to come and get you, and I'm sure this won't be the last." Although Tionne was used to my bluntness, I could tell she was still taken aback by my words. "Tionne, I didn't mean to hurt your feelings." I tried to clean it up.

"This time is different, I swear." Tionne mumbled. Based on her previous actions, she realized it was difficult to believe in her, I know she wanted me to.

"What makes this different from the last time you caught his ass butt naked at the studio? What about the time that bitch showed up on your doorstep? No, I've got one better..." I laughed, unaware of my friend's tears. "What about the time he had a threesome with those two sisters and both of their asses claimed he was the father of their children?" I could go on for days. Dallas was a wild card for sure.

"He burned me." Tionne cried; I almost wrecked the car, barely missing a pedestrian as I ran the red light.

"He did what!?"

"He gave me Chlamydia." Tionne admitted sadly.

"Oh girl, you scared me. I thought you had something much worse." I breathed a sigh of relief. The thought of my best friend being taken out of the world by her no-good husband really shook me up.

"I'm sorry Tionne, are you okay?"

"I'm good now. The doctor gave me a prescription last week." She wiped her eyes. "I know I've said over and over I was leaving but this time is different, I swear. There was something about the doctor's office calling to tell me that my results came back positive for something and to get in the office as soon as possible that shook me up."

Tionne looked out of the window. "What if it was AIDS?"

"Thank God it's not." I patted her shoulder. I could only imagine how Tionne was feeling.

"It was a wakeup call for me though. If that bastard wants to play Russian roulette with his life, that's his business. I won't let him kill me in the process."

"Well for your sake, I hope if ever the day comes that he persuades you to go home, that you remember this day and those words."

"You don't have to worry. I'm done with Dallas Foster aka Black Bishop and all the bullshit that comes with both those muthafuckas." Tionne shook her head. I'm certain she never imagined marrying a celebrity came with so much drama; none of us did. I'm sure people tried to warn her but she was blinded by young love.

"Good thing you don't have any children, it makes the breakup easier." I said thinking of my own situation. If ever I found the strength to leave Jason, Jelly would be the one to suffer. "I can't imagine having to share my baby between two homes on weekends, summer vacations, and holidays."

"I'm ready to just start over with my life, Z. God is giving me a second chance and I want to run with it."

"Where do you go from here?" I asked. "What's your plan B?" From what I knew about Tionne, she didn't have any education beyond high school and had never held a job.

"I don't know. I was thinking about starting an interior design company but it depends on what my lawyer says today. Hopefully, I'll get enough in the divorce settlement for start up money."

"That's a good idea." My girl was a beast when it came to decorating; her home was proof of that. She had even done Jelly's nursery last year as a gift and a thank you for us choosing her as the godmother.

"In order for it to be successful, I'll have to take some business classes and drum up some clientele." She began to ramble.

"Running a business is hard work but I know you'll do great."

"Hopefully, I can get enough start-up money though. If I can't, then I don't know what I'll do." Tionne looked worried.

"Everything will be alright. I know you'll get more than enough money in the settlement T."

"I signed a prenup." Tionne blurted out before looking down at the floor.

"What!"

"I know, I know."

"Maybe there's a loophole or something." I wanted to stop the car and ask her what the hell she was thinking but now wasn't the time.

"I hope so." Tionne smacked her lips. "I thought we would be together forever. So it didn't seem right to plan my divorce before we planned our wedding."

Nearly an hour later, we made it through rush hour traffic and arrived at the law office of Marsha Whitehead, attorney-at-Law. The place was gigantic with oversized furniture, hardwood floors, chandeliers, and oil paintings. It stood four stories tall! "Mrs. Whitehead will see you now." The receptionist announced after approaching us in the second floor lobby.

As we followed her, I eyed Tionne closely; she was a nervous wreck. "It'll be okay, T." I grabbed her hand and held onto it tightly.

"Ladies come on in and have a seat." Marsha greeted from her chair.

"Thanks for meeting with me on such short notice." Tionne reached over to shake her lawyer's hand.

"Anything for you, Mrs. Foster." Marsha grabbed a few documents from a folder. "Let's get straight to it, okay." She waited for Tionne to agree before continuing. "Okay, I read over the prenuptial agreement you signed before marrying Mr. Foster. My findings were rather shocking if I may." She pushed the black frames up onto her nose. "Without going word for word, the summary of this document states that you are entitled to absolutely nothing."

"What about the house?" I interjected.

"Mrs. Foster did not put her name on the deed." Marsha looked down at the paperwork. "Nor did she sign off on either of the luxury vehicles, vacation properties, yacht, or jet. Furthermore, she is not included as a partner in Mr. Foster's business."

"So there isn't any mention of spousal support or anything?" I had to speak up for Tionne who was silent.

"Spousal support would have only been granted if Mrs. Foster had given Mr. Foster a child." Marsha removed her glasses.

"So I get nothing? Absolutely nothing?" Tionne shook her head. "It was me who helped build his empire brick by brick. It was my got damn blood, sweat, and tears!" She hit the corner of Marsha's desk in rage.

"Tionne, did you at least put something up for a rainy day?" I asked.

"No." She mumbled as the realization of her situation hit her like a brick wall. Marsha looked at me and I looked at my friend. Both of us had encountered many women like Tionne, who were so busy living the glamorous life they forgot that fairytales aren't real.

Chapter Fifteen
Diamond

Seeing Duck the other night had me shook. Everywhere I went I couldn't help but feel as if he was following and watching me. It had gotten so bad that I barely left the house. All I wanted to do was lay up under Ken. I realize that I needed to put a plan in motion ASAP. Duck was serious about his two million dollars which is why I was scared shitless. Back in the day, I'd known him to body many people. Therefore, killing me wouldn't be a problem, which is why I put on my game face and did what I do best–grind by any means necessary.

"Lick my ass Diamond." Stewart McKinnon begged with his legs spread eagle up in the air. Instantly, my heart dropped down to my stomach.

"Don't you like this head daddy?" I continued licking all around his wrinkled balls in disgust. His penis was so small that it wouldn't stay in my mouth which his why his sack got all of the attention.

"I haven't had it licked in a while." Stewart begged. He was an old television producer with paper. We used to trick a while back whenever his wife was out of town. Stewart normally had odd requests but this was, by far, the most ridiculous of them all.

"I don't lick ass!"

"But I'm in need Diamond."

"What's it worth to you?" With my index finger, I traced small circles around his anus at an attempt to tease him. Watching him get excited had me about throw up.

"How much more do you want?" He looked down at me.

"Give me another three grand and I'll lick your asshole dry!" I sounded more excited than I actually was. Ass licking wasn't something I enjoyed at all but it did bring in the money.

"Damn it! You want three grand on top of the five I just gave you?"

"You know how this works. Give me what I want and you'll get what you need." I made a show of licking my elongated tongue around my lips.

"Shit!" He gushed, "deal!" Stewart spread his legs so far back that I heard his thigh bones crack.

Closing my eyes, I extended my tongue and dug into the brown hole below his nut sack. Inside was moist, warm, and very loose which meant Stewart had received more than a tongue up his duke chute. The mere thought of his bisexual activities repulsed me. "Damn, I missed you Diamond." Stewart was in la-la land after only five minutes of ecstasy.

"I missed you too." I said while pulling my tongue out of his ass and putting it back into my mouth. The taste of some kind of cream was left behind so I casually grabbed a throw pillow from the bed and ran my tongue across it. Stewart slowly brought his legs down and went to retrieve his trousers lying across the footboard. Leisurely, he pulled out a few bills and placed them in my hand.

"I added another five hundred just because you were a good sport about it." Stewart handed me the money before slipping on his pants. "I take it you remember the way out right?"

"Yes, I remember. See you next time." I nodded and grabbed my purse. On my way out of the bedroom, I caught a glimpse of a tube of Preparation H on the nightstand. The cream residue I tasted was the ass ointment. It took everything in me not to cuss his trifling ass out; instead, I decided to get even.

Once downstairs, I took my time about letting myself out because I knew the place was empty. Going from room to room, I searched for anything of value that I could sell in the streets. Stewart was in his seventies so most of his belongings were old. However, a quick rummage in the kitchen uncovered several 14k gold plates, saucers, and cups. Swiftly, I grabbed as many as I could then made a B-line for the door. I'm pretty sure I looked like a fool running down the street toward my whip with an arm full of dishes. Even so, if I took them to the hood, I knew I could flip them for a small profit. At this point, something was better than nothing. I needed all I could get before Duck came looking for his dough.

Chirp! I hit the lock on the red BMW and watched the trunk rise. Hastily, I unloaded my stolen items then prepared to hop in and take off. But as soon as I closed the trunk, I was scared shitless. "Still up to your old tricks I see."

"Duck, you've got to stop popping up like that for real." I grabbed my heart.

"Just checking up on you to see about my bread that's all." He smirked.

"Nigga, you gave me two weeks remember?" I smacked my lips and pushed past him.

"Oh I remember but you best not forget." Duck lifted his navy Polo shirt to reveal a large caliber gun tucked into the waistband of his jeans. My stomach did a backflip. There was no doubt that if I didn't come through with the money, my ass would end up in a ditch.

Buzz. Buzz. The sound of my phone caused him and I both to look down at my purse. With both eyes on Duck, I reached down and grabbed it.

"Hello. Hey baby." Shit, it was Ken. "Uh, I'm just leaving the mall."

"Get my fucking money Diamond or else." Duck backed away after patting his stomach. I watched as he hustled over to the waiting Ford Mustang and drove off.

"Who was that?" Ken asked.

"Nobody baby. I miss you." I tried to play it cool while stepping into my ride and starting the engine. "I hate that your game is away tonight but I'll be watching boo."

"I know you're my number one cheerleader." Ken spoke over the chatter of his loud ass teammates. "Look baby, I have to go but I wanted to tell you that mom dukes is having a big birthday party back home in Alabama next week. I want you to get with Lyric and go shopping. It's going to be a big weekend."

"Ok, I'll call her tomorrow. Have a good game." Hitting the end button on the screen, I rested my head on the headrest for a second. The thought of going to Alabama scared the shit out of me for two reasons. Foremost, I wasn't thrilled at all about meeting "mom dukes." Second, I needed all the time I could get to obtain Duck's loot. Although it was only for a weekend, that was too long to be off my hustle.

Just as I opened my eyes, I saw Stewart emerge from his house. His head swiveled from side-to-side like he was searching for someone. I knew he couldn't have missed the dishes yet but that didn't stop me from getting the fuck out of dodge. About an hour later, I pulled up in East Hollywood, a sketchy part of Tinseltown. There were hood niggas and Latinos on just about every other corner. Prostitutes strutted like peacocks along with the occasional homeless person on a stroll with a buggy full of shit.

"Damn Diamond, where you been?" Lil Sonto nodded from the curb. He was the 11-year-old son of my friend, Grace, although his ass acted like he was twenty-two.

"Sonto, you better watch your mouth boy." I

smiled before popping the trunk and grabbing the goods. Grace was the number one booster on her side of town. If you wanted to buy anything, you called Grace, if you wanted to sell anything, you called Grace.

"I don't believe my eyes." Grace stepped from behind the rod iron gate on her front door, wearing couchie cutters, fish net stockings, knee boots, and a black button down shirt. People in California dressed weird to me. "Bitch gets with a ball player and forget about her people!" Grace shouted to no one in particular.

"Never that. I've just been busy." I leaned in to kiss her check since my arms were too full for a hug.

"Miss me with that bullshit." Grace reached into her pocket to retrieve a pack of cigarettes. "Nah, I'm just fucking with you. You know you're my girl." She lit the cigarette before taking some of the dishes from my hand and looking them over. "Nice."

"I need top dollar. What you think you can

get for them?" I watched her inspect the plates like she was a genuine appraiser.

"They're good and heavy." She turned them on the back. "Fourteen karat I see."

"You know I wouldn't bring you no average dishes." I laughed.

"I'll give you two grand for the whole set."

"Deal!" Two grand sounded like music to my ears. I didn't even try to wheel and deal.

"Come on in." Grace headed back into her rundown home with me following suit.

Once inside, I sat my load down on the coffee table and took a seat on the torn pleather sofa. The place needed to be cleaned severely. There were food containers, pop bottles, glasses, and several ash trays cluttering up the joint amongst other things. "Don't mind the mess." Grace made a show of trying to get some laundry off the sofa.

"Girl, I know your house is the party house." I laughed. Grace's place was a revolving door for some of Los Angeles' most treacherous residents. I loved my girl but I would never be caught dead over here after dark.

"Let me grab your money then we can catch up." With an arm full of clothing, she retreated toward the back of the house.

While she was gone, I noticed several pictures on the mantel above the fireplace. My eyes scanned each one until they rested on a food scale with a Ziploc bag full of vials. Curiosity pulled me from my seat to get a closer look. My brother had been in the dope game for so long that I knew the vials were filled with heroin–the most deadly and addictive drug on the market. "Got damn." I mumbled. The bag had to be filled with over one hundred vials. Performing a quick tabulation in my head, I knew there was at least twenty thousand dollars sitting here begging me to take it.

"This dumb ass safe is acting up again, Diamond. Give me a minute." Grace called from the backroom.

"Take your time, girl!" I yelled back before grabbing the Ziploc and pouring a few vials into my purse.

"Grace! What you got to eat; I'm starving?" A large, Hispanic man burst through the front door completely catching me off guard. Instinctively, I forced the whole bag of heroin into my purse and took a seat. There was no way for me to put the shit back now.

"Your big ass is always looking for food. You need to be running from the dinner table." Grace walked back into the living room with a smile. "Diamond, this is my boo, Neho. Neho, this is my girl, Diamond, the one I was telling you about."

"What's up." He nodded his head then started toward the kitchen.

"Don't mind him girl. He's much friendlier once he eats." With a laugh, she handed over the money.

"Thanks Grace." I folded the bills then stuck them in my back pocket. After all, there was no way I could open my purse in front of her.

"So tell me what it's like?" Grace flopped down beside me.

CELEBRITY WIVES ASSOCIATION

"What's what like?"

"Being a celebrity's wife?"

"Well I'm not a wife yet but it's cool for the most part." I shrugged. Grace and I once swung from the same pole. It felt weird to be bragging about how my life turned out for the better when she was still in the same situation.

"Maybe one day I'll meet my prince and he'll whisk me away from the ghetto too." She looked back at Neho who wasn't paying us any attention.

"It'll happen Grace. If I find another prince, I'll send him your way." I winked.

"Well until then, I'll be here selling dogs, dishes, and dope or whatever I can just to feed my son." Grace laughed but I knew she was serious. "Nah, but for real I'm happy for you, Diamond." She reached over to hug me. Instantly, I felt bad. The heroin I'd just stolen was ultimately taking food from Sonto's mouth.

"Thanks girl." I stood and grabbed my purse. "Next time you come out to my neck of the woods, we'll hang for the day okay." To be honest, I had no plans on seeing Grace or anyone from my past life ever again.

"Why are you leaving? You just got here."

"I promised to meet Ken for dinner." Truth was the sun was going down which meant it was time to get the fuck back to my side of town.

Chapter Sixteen
Jasmine

It had been twenty-four hours and I was still raging. "How could he? I mean it was one thing to accuse me of cheating but it was another thing to do it in a room full of people while pulling my hair!" I screamed into my phone.

"Wait 'til this nigga get back in the D! I got heat for nigga's like that!" Stacey yelled.

"I swear I'm done with this shit! I can't take it anymore, Stace. The killing part is the whole time the nigga was in my face yelling, his breath was smelling like pussy! He fucked the bitch and ate her pussy while my dumb ass waited in the lobby." I shook my head and wiped at a tear. I was dressed in a peach, Juicy Couture sweat suit with gold sandals, gold, hoop earrings and my real hair slicked back into a ponytail. After leaving that nightmare of an event yesterday, I checked into a Holiday Inn that was about eight miles away from our room at the W. I paid the concierge to transport my luggage over here and begged her not to tell King where I was. I took a long shower, washed my hair, and removed my tracks. I turned off my cell phone and refused to watch television or turn on the radio. I knew that it wouldn't take long for my business to hit the airways, so I needed time to reflect before it did.

My only reason for turning my phone on today was to check in with my mom and Jordan then book a flight home. The minute my signal came in, my shit began to blow up. There were fifty messages, most of which were not from King. They were from his publicist Danielle, my mom, and a few other relatives, who had more than likely, saw that crazy shit on TMZ or something. "Do you want me to come out there?" Stacey asked, grabbing my attention.

"No, I'm cool. I'm leaving here first thing in the morning. Tonight, I'm just going to chill here at the hotel. I might call Amelia to see if she's available for dinner." I said thinking about my good friend that lived in Cali. Amelia was the ex-girlfriend of Kold Hart, another rapper in the game.

She left his ass last year after finding out he had gotten two people pregnant during their relationship. Since then, she's made a name for herself in the fashion industry both as a model and designer.

"Okay that's cool. Well tell Amelia hello for me and I'll see you tomorrow." We ended the call then I walked onto the balcony to catch some sun. It was beautiful outside; it felt good to have some alone time. No King, no press, no Jordan, no anything. I didn't have to be a mom, wife, nurse, teacher, and maid all while in six inch heels and smiling for the cameras. Actually, it felt good to be makeup free with no hair extensions. This reminded me of the old days; I was enjoying this time away from my real life.

I sat down on the tan, lounge chair, put on my Dolce and Gabbana shades then dialed my mother. "Hello?"

"Hey mama, how are you and Jordan?" I asked.

"Hey yourself baby girl. We're good, but

how are you baby?" I could tell by the tone in her voice she already knew what was up.

"So you've heard, huh?"

"Yes baby, it's all over the place. What happened; what did you do to make him that mad?" She said out of concern, but I stopped and stared at the phone in disbelief.

"Mama, why would you think it was me?" I asked bewildered. My mama has always had my back; there must've been a good reason for her to ask what I had done.

"Well..." She let her word hang in the air.

"Well nothing mama. I didn't do anything to him. He ran off to go fuck some actress and left me in the lobby of the hotel. A man came up to me with a business card for King. He said he wanted to cast him in his next movie, so I put the card in my purse. The man walked away, King walked up and went ape shit on me, pulling my hair and dragging me." I waited for her to speak.

"Jasmine, are you sure that's what happened?"

"Am I sure? I know you didn't ask me if I was sure. I was there and so was about a thousand other people, go ask them." I was beyond pissed and about to hang the phone up.

"Calm down, honey. I only asked because the report that I watched didn't mention anything about him putting his hands on you. It said that you had too much to drink and openly flirted with some man at the premier. It also said that King was really embarrassed because you were sloppy and falling all over the place." She paused and cleared her throat. "Baby, they even showed pictures of you on the floor trying to cover your private parts."

I gasped at what she was saying. "I swear on my son that was not what went down. This is all Danielle's doing. That bitch!" I spat. "Look mama, I have to go. Kiss my son and tell him I'll be there tomorrow." I tapped the end button on my phone screen then immediately dialed Danielle.

"Danielle Crawford." She answered on the second ring.

"Bitch, why in the fuck would you spin the

story like that!? You know that's not what
happened!" I yelled.

"Excuse me, but I'm no one's bitch." She
cut into me. "First of all Mrs. James, let me remind
you that I don't work for you, I work for Mr. James.
My best interest lies with him." She said as a matter
of fact.

"You're dirty Danielle. You know what he
did to me yet you sold me out. Protecting him only
makes him think its okay to do the things he does
and you're foul for that." I was about to cry because
I was hurt.

"Jasmine, let me tell you something.
Protecting him only means I get paid and so do you!
If King gets locked up or looks like the bad guy in
the press, no one eats. Do you understand that?"
She attempted to scold me like a child. "So what?
We had to make it look like you were the one out-
of-pocket. So what? We had to pay people to back
up our story and so fucking what your feelings are
hurt. At the end of the day, we averted a disaster
that could've ended King's career. You have to learn

that taking one for the team will happen every once in a while. You have to do your part and play your position if it keeps food on the table, clothes on your back–designer clothes I might add–and pays for your son's medical bills!" She ranted.

"Don't say anything about Jordan!" I screamed as the tears rolled down my face. Danielle sighed.

"Jasmine, off the record, King is the biggest asshole I know. Do I condone the shit that he does to you–no, I don't. But it's a job and I do it well because it pays my bills. Am I sorry that this happened to you–yes, I am. However, you stay and continue to except his bullshit time-after-time. You're a beautiful young woman with so much to offer this world. I think its time for you to do you and leave his ass. Then again, if I know you like I believe I do, your ass ain't going nowhere." Her words hit me like a ton of bricks. "Now if you don't mind Jasmine, I have to take another call. I'll speak with you later, goodbye."

Chapter Seventeen

Lyric

Within the week, I had received two blessings. The first one came from Ken, the second came from Damien. He secured the role in the movie he auditioned for and was waiting for them to start production. The leading role came with the wage of one hundred fifty thousand dollars but due to his track record, he had to wait until the movie wrapped before he would see a dime of his earnings. Therefore, your girl was back on the move trying to find new ways to rob Peter to pay Paul.

"You know Lyric, you would be great for this show I'm doing." China, my client looked down at me as I pinned the hem on her skirt. She was the girlfriend of Young Guap, a southern rapper new on the scene.

"What show?" I asked without really wanting to know. There was so much shit on my mind that whatever she was saying sounded like Morse code.

"Celebs And The Women Who Love Them."

She stated nonchalantly.

"Oh, is it new? I've never heard of that one." After finishing the hem, I grabbed the portable steamer and went about tackling the wrinkles in her blouse.

"Girl, it's only the hottest franchise in the history of reality TV. Where have you been?"

"Apparently, under a rock." I laughed. "I'm always working, so I never get to watch television."

"That's why you should do the show...for your company. The cameras follow you around almost all day. You could show the world that some celebrity wives actually do work while at the same time, promoting your shit." China, had it all figured out. "Not to mention getting that reality check." She rubbed her stiletto nails together.

"If you don't mind me asking, how much are those checks?" Now that we were talking money, she had my attention.

"Everybody is paid a different amount but they start you off at fifty G's. The more you bring to the table, the more money you make. Hell, I plan on being the biggest bitch on the network."

"Straight up?"

"Yeah girl!" She smacked her lips.

"I don't think I could act a fool on national television." I could just imagine my mother cringing.

"Fuck all that, I'm trying to get paid. I don't care nothing about what people think." She laughed before slipping into the McQueens resting before her. "Some of those bitches clear at least a quarter million or better."

"Really?"

"Girl, you need to get on this train before it pulls off." China made train noises with her mouth.

"What's the producer's number?" I knew China had probably trumped up the pay scale but it was still worth making the call. Who could pass up a paycheck and free publicity?

"No need to call her. She should be arriving any minute. Today, they're shooting my scenes. That's why I needed you to style me. I can't be on TV looking busted." She said just as the doorbell rang. While she went to answer her door, I started packing up my things.

As I pondered my future in television, a barrage of people swarmed the place with lighting and cameras. "Move that atrocious sofa now and put the fuckin' cat up." A lady yelled from behind the biggest pair of sunglasses I'd ever seen. "I hate cats!"

"Sorry Linda, I didn't know." China apologized.

"Now you do, so please don't let it happen again." Linda removed the sunglasses from her face then placed them on top of her head. "Who are you?" She stared me up and down.

"Linda, this is my friend Lyric, she's a stylist. We thought she may be a good fit for the show. Lyric, this is Linda Schmidt, the genius behind the CATWWLT kraze."

"What is CATWWLT?" I hated to be rude but I didn't know what in the world that meant.

"Celebs And The Women Who Love Them," China whispered. Almost everyone in the room gasped like I was supposed to know. "Lyric is a virgin to all of this which is why she would be perfect." China laughed.

"I see." Linda continued to stare me down. "You have five minutes to brief me on why you want a spot on my show, starting now!" She snapped her fingers and I rolled my eyes.

"First off, who said I wanted a spot on your show?" I didn't like her attitude.

"What Lyric meant to say was she's not only a celebrity wife but she's a mom and a mogul. She wants to share the ins and outs of her life with the world." China added. If the girl wasn't trying to be the next big reality bitch, she could've definitely had a job in PR.

"Boring!" Linda barked. "I'm already over it." She yawned.

"Fuck it then!" I barked back. I was already tired of her dramatics.

"Her husband is Damien Robertson!" China shouted as a last ditch effort to secure my spot on the show. Immediately, Linda's eyes raised and a smile that resembled the Grinch's took over the frown she once possessed.

"Damien Robertson, as in the Damien Robertson who ran through LAX butt naked a few months ago?" Linda recalled a situation I wished I could forget. During one of his drug binges, my husband showed up at the airport high and acting erratic. Police tried to detain him but he evaded them. While running, Damien thought it was a good idea to strip down to his birthday suit. He was later arrested for public indecency. "Mrs. Robertson, I would love to have you aboard." She extended a hand my way. Quite naturally, I hesitated before reciprocating the gesture.

"Linda, I want some time to think before I sign on." I really needed to talk things over with Damien before making a decision. I also had to think about how this could potentially affect my children.

"The spot won't be open for long, Mrs. Robertson." Linda threatened like that would make me sign up any sooner.

"Look lady, I'm not one of these little girls around here begging for a chance at fame and fortune. I've been there, done that, and wrote the fucking book about it. I don't need no D-list celebrity status. I've been walking on red carpets since you were probably somebody's intern. Google me bitch!" With those words, I grabbed my shit then headed for the door.

On the way to my car, I made a mental note to call China later and apologize. I really didn't mean to offend her with my jabs especially when she was trying to help me out. "Lyric, wait up!" China called from her door.

"I'm sorry about all that." I walked up to her as she struggled not to scuff her borrowed McQueens running down the driveway.

"Girl, forget all of that! Linda just grabbed her checkbook and told me to give you this." She flashed a three hundred thousand dollar check in my face. "I didn't even get that much!"

"As sexy as it looks I can't take it."

"Why not?" China frowned.

"I'm just not with this." I shook my head. Money was the evil and I wasn't down with making deals with the devil.

"Just take it and I'll tell her you'll think about it." China forced the check into my hand before turning to head back into the spotlight.

Chapter Eighteen

Jasmine

Four hours after speaking with Danielle, her words were still heavy on my mind. I replayed the conversation over and over until there was a knock at my room door. I looked at my watch; my girl Amelia was right on time. "Here I come girl." I called out as I grabbed my Dooney & Burke hobo bag off the cream sofa. We had plans for dinner and taking in the newest Tyler Perry movie.

"What's up diva!?" Amelia shouted from the door as I opened it. My girl was fierce in a denim halter top and matching capris. Her makeup was flawless and her body was in great shape. As a matter of fact, I've never seen Amelia look so good. I didn't know if it was the new blonde hair or the peaceful look on her face but my girl looked great. She was standing there with a bag of carryout that smelled delicious in her right hand and her custom, LV bag along with a movie rental bag in the left.

"Girl, you must've sensed that I wasn't

really feeling the crowds." I took the carryout bag from her and let her pass.

"Yeah girl, I've been there and I definitely understand." She put the movies down then embraced me with a warm hug. It felt really good to have a friend right now, especially since Stacey was back in the D.

"Did you see that shit on the blogs? They got your girl looking bad." I tried to laugh it off.

"Girl, you know I ain't no blog reader, but my girl, Tina, was at the premier. She told me the real deal. She said after Danielle and her team got through with the place, nobody could recall what had actually happened. All the A and B-list celebrities didn't give a fuck. The C and D-list celebrities were just happy to be invited to the premier. Child, and the fans were all too geeked to do what Danielle asked as long as they got a KJ autograph and twenty-five dollars in gas money." Amelia cracked up laughing and I did too.

"Girl, I didn't know fame would be like this. I thought me and King would be different, you know. Back in Detroit, when we were broke and nobodies, we had each other's back. I thought it would be the same way once we came up out the hood." I said popping the lid on the Thai containers. My girl had hooked me up with my favorite, Pad Thai with broccoli, the number twenty sauce and two egg rolls with extra house sauce for dipping.

"It's like Biggie said, Mo' money Mo' problems. These niggas get money and they forget who had their backs when they didn't have a pot to piss in or a window to throw it out of." She grabbed her food and sat down Indian style on the floor by the couch. There was a dinette set right there but I guess she wanted to go old school, so I plopped down and joined her.

"I know that's right. I'm just tired of pretending. I'm so over this lifestyle it's not even funny." I took a bite of my egg roll. "Fuck the house, the money, the cars, fame and fuck King too!" I snapped.

"You sound like me when I left Gordon... I'm sorry, "Kold Hart" she made air quotes with her fingers. "He had been my man for nine years. All I wanted was a ring and a baby but he didn't want to give me either. Then out of nowhere while we were in bed watching the Kardashians, an alert scrolled across the bottom of the screen. It read that congratulations were in order to the D.C. rapper Kold Hart and his longtime girlfriend, Shaniya on the birth of their daughter. It also reported it was the rapper and model's second child." She rolled her eyes.

"Oh my god girl! What did you do?" I asked with a mouth full of noodles.

"I didn't say shit that night, but the next day he left to do a video shoot and my ass called all my girls. Within eight hours, I had purchased a new condo, moved my shit out of his house and into my own. I also deposited two million dollars into my bank account from his." She laughed. "Child, just as that nigga was pulling into the gate, me and five of my friends were riding out of the gate, waving and blowing the horns on all his muthafuckin cars. Trina was in the Land Rover, Jessie was in the

Lamborghini, Daisha was pushing the Rolls Royce,
Vicky was in the Phantom, Toni was in the
Mercedes, and I flexed hard in the Maybach." We
slapped fives and I laughed hysterically.

"Bitch, you got balls. I wish I was like that."
I laid back on the floor and daydreamed.

"Just wait until you've had enough, you
might be surprised at what you'll do." Amelia laid
down beside me. She must've been full because she
unloosened her Hermes belt and undid the top
button on her capris. The girl was a solid size 2 but
she ate like a man.

"I told you I'm done with him. When I get
home, I'm moving out and I mean that." I looked
over at her and she rolled her eyes.

"Child, you ain't at your breaking point
yet." She shook her head.

"How do you know?" I questioned.

"Because if you were, we wouldn't be here
eating Thai and talking shit! Your ass would've
been on the first thing smoking back to Detroit. You
would've been on the phone with lawyers and a real

estate agent, not lounging around with me like life is beautiful." She put her hand over mine. "But Jasmine that's okay. Like I said, you'll know when you've had enough because you'll end up surprising yourself." She winked.

The rest of the evening went swell. We watched *Diary of a Mad Black Woman* and *Waiting to Exhale*. I guess Amelia was dropping hints. She had left about an hour ago and I was about to get into the tub. With a five a.m. flight in the morning, I needed to retire early tonight.

As soon as my big toe touched the scalding hot water, there was a knock at the door. *Of course!* I thought. I wrapped up in the hotel's plush white robe and headed for the door. I glanced around the room to see if Amelia had forgotten anything. "Who is it?" I called out.

"It's King, open up." I froze and stopped dead in my tracks.

"King, please leave." I said nervously.

"Jazzy, open the door. I need to talk to you." His voice sounded shaky. I tiptoed up to the door and peered through the peep hole. I was at a lost for words when I saw that he was crying. In all the years that I've been with King, I've never seen him cry.

"Talk to me about what? I said with my back pressed against the door.

"Baby, I'm sorry, so sorry. I'm in trouble baby, please open the door." He whimpered. Taking a deep breath, I turned the lock then pulled the door open. King was still in his suit from yesterday. He looked a mess. I could sense that something was definitely wrong. He took a step forward and fell into my arms, sobbing like a baby.

"King, what's the matter?" I was starting to panic; I had never seen him like this.

"Jasmine, I fucked up and I'm sorry. Please forgive me baby; please forgive me." He begged. I guided him over to the sofa.

"It'll be okay, whatever it is." I said now wiping my own tears. I didn't know why I was crying but the shit was contagious.

"No baby, you've got to say you forgive

me." He looked up at me.

Choosing my words carefully, I said, "King, I forgive but I can't forget that easily. You put your hands on me and publicly humiliated me. To top it off, you let Danielle shit on me in the media."

"Baby, I swear I will never put my hands on you again and I didn't let Danielle do anything. You know Danielle, I wasn't answering my phone and neither were you, so she took control of the situation." He sniffled and finally stopped crying. "Jazzy, I know you're the only one that has my back besides God and moms, so it's time for me to come clean. I need to tell you something." He looked into my eyes. I stood from the couch on defense mode.

"King, it bettin not be another woman or no babies."

"Jazzy, it ain't shit like that. I came here to confess that for the past two years, I've been sniffing cocaine." He confided.

"You've been what?" I cut him off mid-sentence.

"That's why I've been acting strange. I need

help and didn't realize it 'til yesterday when I did what I did. I had just done a line with Melissa Valentine and was blowed out of my mine. I didn't realize what I'd done until last night when I was coming down from my high." He began to sniff again. "Jazzy, I've been trying to hide my habit, but it's taking over and starting to control me."

"How did you let this happen?" I said in disbelief. King never even smoked weed now he was sniffing coke.

"It all started when I was doing my junior album, *Money Over Everything*. I was up late, sleeping 'bout two hours a day for two months straight. Right after that, we left for promotional road shows. State after state, it was the same story, radio interviews in the morning, magazine spreads late afternoon, sound checks before performances, and of course, fans think you on some other shit if you ain't at the after-party. It just became too much! One day, some industry cat came through and told me all of my problems would be solved. He gave me a sample and from there I was hooked. Once a month turned into every two weeks which ended up being every day. Now I can't function without it."

I saw the pain in his eyes and felt his sadness in my heart. I couldn't imagine what King had been going through but it did shed light on a lot of things. "Jazzy, I need help." He put his head down in my lap. "Can you help me?" He asked.

"You know I'm gonna help baby. Now let's get you cleaned up." I helped him remove his suit and step into the bath water that was still waiting for me. I washed my man and told him everything would be okay. I also recommended checking into rehab but he refused.

"If I have to go cold turkey, I want to do it at home with you by my side." He said. I was leery but as we lay in bed that night, he reassured me he was going to kick this habit and I believed him.

The flight home was wonderful. I was too excited to be back on Michigan soil. As promised, my girl Stacey was front and center, waiting curbside to pick me up. I ignored the scowl on her face when she saw King beside me as I'm sure she ignored my frown at the sight of her sister in the front seat riding shot gun. She popped her trunk so we could put our bags inside. After tipping the gentleman that helped bring our luggage to the car, we got into the back of the car. Without a word exchanged between anyone, not even Stace and I, she pulled off and headed in the direction of our home.

"How was your trip? Did anything interesting happen?" Tracey snickered. I caught a glimpse of Stacey in the rearview and rolled my eyes. Why did she bring this hood bugger anyway? I reached over and squeezed King's hand. He smiled and continued to peer out of the window.

Within thirty minutes, we were at my gate and I was punching the code. "Thank God." I mumbled under my breath. Stacey drove up the circular driveway and stopped right in front of the steps between two, stone, lion head statues.

"Thanks girl for the ride." I reached in the car window and tried to hug her but she was stiff.

"Jasmine, I thought you were done with

this?" She whispered as King retrieved our luggage.

"It's a long story; I promise I'll call you in a few days." I explained.

"A few days?" She repeated.

"I'll explain everything in a day or two. Please just understand." I begged. With that, she put her car in gear, pulled off, and left me standing there.

"Jazzy, I told you I don't like that hoe!" King hollered. I simply shook my head because the feelings between the two of them were definitely mutual.

I stepped inside the foyer and was greeted by the aroma of something from down south. My mother was from Alabama and could throw down on some soul food. "Mama, what are you cooking?" I just knew it was her in the kitchen.

"I made some fried catfish, smothered pork chops, string beans, collard greens, baked sweet potatoes, macaroni and cheese, potato salad, corn muffins, and hot water bread." Removing her apron, she waved her hand like a model across the spread of food sitting along the granite countertops.

"Why did you make so much food?" I asked while kissing Jordan. He was at the table in his special wheelchair/highchair.

"Well baby girl." She smiled. "Me and Jordan think you guys need some alone time. I know you can't boil water, so I wanted to make enough for a few days. Jordan is going to stay with me so mommy and daddy can relax. Isn't that right J-man?" She tickled Jordan, causing him to laugh. Before our flight this morning, I called and told her everything about the cocaine and how King wanted to kick the habit without rehab. She probably figured things could potentially get ugly and Jordan didn't need to be present.

"Thanks Wanda." King hugged my mother.

"See ya later Jordan." He waived at our son and I swallowed hard. He had never hugged or kissed Jordan, it was almost like he was scared to touch him. I thanked my mom again for everything and walked them to the car. After kissing Jordan one last time, I waved them off. Turning to face the house, I released an audible breath. The next few days were going to be challenging. I rolled up the sleeves on my Yves St. Laurent blazer, prepared for war. I was going to bring the man I fell in love with back to life because I was tired of this impersonator.

Chapter Nineteen

Tionne

The meeting at the lawyer's office had me so far down in the dumps that Zuri had to call in reinforcements to try and cheer me up. "Divas!" My friend Lyric sang as she approached our table. We were sitting at the back booth of Charlie's Place, a gourmet diner not far from my hotel.

"Hey Girl." Zuri stood for a hug but I remained seated. The three margaritas that I'd guzzled thirty minutes earlier were playing tricks with my vision and balance.

"Damn T, you started the party without me?" She took a seat beside me then wrapped her arm around my shoulder. "Girl, it's going to be alright."

"I gave him everything I had to build his empire but I get nothing in the end." I know the other day my mission was to leave with what I'd come with. However, after a few nights of thinking, I remembered that Dallas had also come with nothing. We built everything we had together. Why didn't I deserve a parting gift? "Y'all, I didn't even want half. I just wanted something to get me by until I could start my own company and make my own money."

"Do you have any private accounts, secret stashes, or anything that you could sell?" Lyric asked.

"No." I shook my head before grabbing the remainder of Zuri's cocktail and taking it to the head. "I can't believe I was such a naïve little bitch who thought my marriage would outlast this industry."

"Tionne, don't beat yourself up." Lyric patted my hand. "We've all played the naïve position a time or two."

"Why is being the wife of a celebrity so got damn hard?" Life was much better when things were simple. "You give a nigga a little fame and fortune and they go crazy."

"I'll toast to that." Zuri raised one of the freshly filled beverages from the trio the waiter had just placed on the table. Lyric and I followed suit.

"Amen!" I swigged my drink then wiped my mouth with the back of my hand.

"Did y'all hear about Jasmine James and KJ?" Lyric asked. "T, that's your girl right?"

"Yeah, she's my people. We actually went to high school together." I nodded. The news feed on my phone had been blowing up all day about the craziness that went down last night. "I tried to give her a call earlier but she won't answer." I just wanted to show her some love since she's so far away from home but I knew firsthand how it was when you didn't feel like being bothered.

"She probably booked the first flight back to Detroit." Zuri looked up from her phone. I guess she was checking out the story. "I know I would have."

"Maybe, I should go home and check on her."

"What? Why would you wanna go there?" Zuri frowned.

"Girl, I saw some pictures online; that place

looks scary as hell." Lyric shook her head.

"First of all, y'all bitches better back up off the D. There are still some nice areas; the media chooses to only show the blighted areas of my city." I loved my birthplace so much that I had a small tat under my left breast that read, *Est. In Detroit.*

"Well you can have the D or whatever you call it. I'll stay my ass right here in sunny California." Lyric laughed.

"Fuck you." I giggled.

"See," Lyric pointed at me. "Detroit breeds them gangstas."

We all burst into laughter.

"Seriously though, I think I'll just call her again." I said suddenly remembering that I no longer had the luxury of booking flights whenever I felt like it. "Besides, she may not feel up to any company right now."

"Poor thing probably needs a vacation." Lyric added.

"I know I need one." I agreed.

"Me too." Lyric raised her glass.

"Well this is perfect timing." Zuri smiled. "I wanted to invite you girls on a trip to Puerto Rico." She sang. "Tionne, if you speak to Jasmine, please extend the invite to her as well. Although I don't really know her, I do know that the CWA has to stick together."

"What's the CWA?" I frowned, trying to figure out the acronym.

"Celebrity Wives Association." Zuri laughed.

"I like that one." Lyric giggled.

"Tramp, don't take my shit and tell people you made it up." Zuri pointed across the table. The alcohol was finally starting to affect them but my ass had been wasted.

"Tell me more about this trip. How many days?" I was excited.

"Girl, I'm talking about five nights on the beach just maxing and relaxing."

Immediately, I noticed Lyric tense up. "How much will it cost?" She asked hesitantly.

"This is an all-expense-paid-trip, boo."

"Are you serious?" I'd known Zuri to buy a bitch a nice bag or a pair of shoes a time or two but never had she treated me and Lyric on a vacation. "Thank you Z!" I jumped up and hugged my girl.

"Don't thank me, thank Jason." Zuri fingered the rim of her class.

"Must be nice to have a husband like that." Lyric mumbled. She didn't really talk to us about her situation with Damien but we'd heard through the grapevine that her money was a little funny lately.

"Don't do that Lyric." Zuri wagged her finger.

"I'm just saying it must be nice to have a fine ass husband, who spoils you, and remains faithful. I mean I got two out of three but you got a blessing." Lyric laughed.

"I said the same thing." I slapped her five, much to Zuri's dismay.

"Y'all bitches don't know half my struggle." Zuri continued playing with the rim of her glass.

"All we know is what we see and damn it

your life looks good from this side of the table."
Lyric raised her hand to her eyebrows then turned
her head from side to side as if she was looking for
something. We all cracked up at her theatrics, even
Zuri but that didn't stop her from throwing us the
middle finger.

"You two bitches are hilarious. Y'all need
your own reality show." I wiped the tears from my
eyes. They had me crying.

"Fuck that! I will never, ever do a reality
show as long as I live." Zuri rolled her eyes. "They
make everyone look like clowns or gangstas and I
ain't either. I have way too much class to sell
myself for a fucking check."

"Yeah, I can't do it either." I shook my head.
"There is no way I could imagine watching my life
play out on television. Could y'all imagine a camera
crew sitting here with us while I'm a drunken
mess." Grabbing Lyric's glass, I tipped it up. "I
could see it now. Under my name would read, *The
Alcoholic*. Nah, I'm good."

"Funny you should mention that." Lyric

went into her clutch and laid a check on the table.

"Who the fuck is Linda Schmidt?" I slurred.

"She's the face behind all the reality television shows we've been bombarded with these past few years." Lyric informed us.

"No you didn't!" Zuri's mouth fell wide-open.

"I didn't, I swear." Lyric raised her hands.

"So how did you get the check?" I asked with my lips twisted.

"I was styling a client who will be on her new show and Linda was there. She gave me a check; I'm supposed to be thinking about it."

"I know she didn't insult you with this chump change!" Zuri snapped. "Besides, I heard Linda Schmidt is bad news. Several of her cast members have filed lawsuits against her company for twisting their words and causing beef that leads to attacks on air by other cast members."

I didn't think more than a quarter million dollars was chump change especially now that I was flat broke but I did agree with Zuri about not doing the show. "I don't think you should do it Lyric. You've kept your private life private all this time. Don't switch up now."

"You're right." Lyric stared at the lump sum shortly before ripping it to pieces and tossing the confetti into her empty glass. "No amount of money is worth jeopardizing my family, my company, or my character." She declared. I knew it was a huge decision for her to make, especially in times of need. Nevertheless, ultimately, she thought with her head and not her purse.

"So anyway, back to my trip! Are y'all bitches down or what?"

"Hell yeah!" Lyric and I sung in unison.

"Let's leave on Monday. The sooner the better."

"Puerto Rico here we come!" I beckoned the waiter for another round of drinks.

Chapter Twenty
Diamond

"Babe, where did you say you were going again?" Ken asked from the shower. He'd been home all day and I was a little irritated. Normally, I loved having my man around, but today I had to shoot some moves. His ass was holding me up.

"I called Lyric. We're going shopping for a few hours." It was a bold face lie but it bought me some time to do what I needed to do.

"Don't spend all my money." Ken laughed.

"Don't worry, I will!" I yelled through the closed door.

"I got a few dollars in my sock drawer, take all of it."

"Thanks boo." I walked over to the drawer and began rummaging. Right away, I spotted a white envelope with several hundreds inside. The outside of the envelope had the amount $17,000 written on it. I was about to close the drawer when I noticed a checkbook. As soon as I grabbed it, Ken's voice boomed from the bathroom.

"I can't wait to show you off to my family. I know my country ass cousins ain't ever seen a chick like you."

"Shit!" I clutched my heart. He'd scared me to death. "I can't either boo." Without delay, I snatched a blank check from the back of his checkbook and tucked it into the back pocket on my jeans. I hated to steal from Ken but desperate times called for desperate measure. Besides, I knew Ken was a multimillionaire. He would hardly miss anything I withdrew from his account. "Be back in a few." I yelled before closing the drawer and making a mad dash to the door.

Once inside of my car, I called my brother. "Hello."

"Dexter, I'm on my way over to your friend's crib now. Are you sure he's legit?"

"Yeah, Omar is a cool dude. I told him you had the goods; he said he would give you twelve thousand." Eddie spoke close into the receiver of his phone.

"Twelve? I need at least twenty!"

"Girl, ain't nobody gon' pay you top dollar for a hookup because then it wouldn't be a hookup." Dex laughed. "Besides, niggas like Omar don't even fuck with people he don't know. He's only doing business with you because you're my sister." When I called Dexter the other day to see how I could get rid of the heroin, he told me about Omar, a big time dope boy he did business with ever now and then.

"I guess it'll have to do. I'm on my way over there now."

"Diamond, please be careful. This shit ain't pretend. These are real niggas you're about to encounter." Dexter warned. My brother had been in the dope game all of my life. By now, he should've known I was used to drugs, guns, police, and killers.

"I'm a big girl. I can handle my own." Without another word, I ended the call then headed over to see Omar.

During the ride, I could see Duck's Charger tailing me from two cars behind. Completely annoyed, I pulled up into the gas station and waited for him to do the same. As soon as he pulled into the parking space beside me, I rolled down my window and let him have it. "I told you to quit fucking following me! You're blowing my cover!"

"And I told you that I keep close watch on my money." Duck grimaced.

"When I get it, I'll be in touch. Until then, back the fuck off!" I rolled up the window, released my foot from the brake and peeled out of there on two wheels. Duck tried to catch up but it was useless. By the time he was back on the street, he couldn't see shit but the dust my car had left behind.

Nearly twenty minutes after losing him, I pulled up to a nice home on a decent street. There was a flower bed, the grass was mowed, and the hedges were trimmed. A nice Cadillac rested in the driveway as well as a few toys. Thinking I had the wrong address, I checked the paper I'd wrote it down on against what I'd put in the GPS. Surprisingly, this was the correct address. Hastily, I grabbed my bag and approached the door. Before I could knock, it swung open. "Yes." The nose of a nine millimeter handgun greeted me.

"Is Omar here?"

"Who wants to know?" The assassin brandishing the weapon was a mixed woman with curly hair and a strong bone structure.

"My name is Diamond." I stared her down. Letting her know I wasn't intimidated by her ice grill or pistol.

"Come on in." She stepped aside, allowing me to enter. "My name is Isis. Omar left an hour ago but he did say you were coming by." She placed the gun behind her back and tucked it into her jeans. "You got the shit?"

"Yeah, right here." I patted my bag. "You got the money."

"It's all here." After she grabbed a large manila envelope from the coffee table, I reached into my purse and handed her the vials still in the Ziploc bag. I watched as Isis peered into the bag and nodded her approval. "It looks good but if it's not, Omar will want all of his money back."

"That shit is fire. Got the dope fiends going crazy in the city." One thing I knew how to do was bluff.

"It better be because Omar don't take kindly to con artists." Isis warned. "The last nigga who tried to pass off some whack shit came up missing and he ain't been found since."

I wanted to check her for using the word nigga but then I remembered she was the bitch holding the gun. "Try it if you don't believe me." I urged, fully praying and hoping the stolen dope was good.

"If need be, we'll be in touch." Isis nodded toward the door. That was my queue to put it in gear and get the hell out of here.

Chapter Twenty-one
Jasmine

After several long days and nights of vomiting, cold sweats, and nightmares, I wished like hell I'd taken Tionne's offer to join her and the other girls on the beach. I really appreciated her offer to come home and check on me too but my hands were full. Being on call all day and night was no easy feat. However, I could finally see the original King James begin to emerge. To say I was grateful would've been an understatement. His whole demeanor had changed in a week. He was more attentive to my needs and had even cooked dinner and catered to me last night. It felt like the old days with no distractions. No industry calls, no blogs to read, and no television to watch. We had taken a vacation from the world and it felt great!

"Jazzy, I want tonight to be special, so pick out your best dress and flyest heels." He lay down on the pool chair next to me and grabbed my hand.

"What's the special occasion?" I smiled.

"Today is the day that I asked you to marry me all those years ago." He winked as I calculated the dates in my head.

"Baby, I can't believe you actually remember that." I was impressed.

"Jazzy, you're my rock, my world, and my foundation. Without you, I'm nothing and I don't want to lose you."

"I'm not going anywhere, King." My voice was unsteady and my hand was trembling.

"Now go take your fine ass upstairs and get ready. I got everything set up in the formal dining room, no peaking."

"Scout's honor." I said with my fingers crossed behind my back. I wasn't promising anything and he knew I was going to peek. I had to see what he had prepared and what gifts were waiting for me.

"Oh my god!" I exclaimed. The sight was breathtaking. King had pulled out all of the stops; I was beaming with excitement. This gesture proved that his love for me hadn't died. There were ten dozen roses in a variety of red, white, and pink scattered around the room. I took notice of all the boxes which were strategically placed in every chair of the twelve-seat dinette set.

"I thought I said no peeking." King said from behind me as he wrapped his strong arms around my waist.

"Baby, can I at least open one." I was as bright-eyed as a kid on Christmas. King walked over to the head seat then pulled the yellow-wrapped box from the chair.

"Only one though. After this one, go upstairs and get ready." He smiled as I pulled on the ribbon. DING. DONG. The sound of the doorbell stole our attention.

"Who could that be? I'll be right back." I said placing my gift down.

"I'll get it. You continue opening your gift and I'll be right back." King placed the box back in my hand then walked off. I tore into the pretty paper and gasped when I saw the Diamond necklace, matching tennis bracelet, and ankle bracelet. They each had Diamond encrusted hearts hanging off of them. The necklace had King's name on the back, the tennis bracelet said Jordan, and the ankle bracelet was blank. *Was King trying to give me a hint that he was ready to have a baby?* The tears began to fall; I couldn't contain myself. Tonight would be the night I would tell him we were expecting.

"King, who was at the door?" I asked when he returned to the dining room.

"It was D-Bo." He said casually but something in his voice concerned me. D-Bo was his bodyguard and right-hand man. He does anything for King; sometimes, that's not a good thing.

"What did he want?" I raised an eyebrow.

"He brought over our flight details for tomorrow." He averted his eyes from me.

"Tomorrow?" I looked at him suspiciously. "Where are you going tomorrow?"

"The label wants to shoot this video for my next single in Atlanta. I should be gone no more than two days." He fumbled with his hands.

"Are you okay?" I finally spit it out because he was acting too awkward.

"Jazz, I'm good girl. Now go upstairs and get ready." He playfully grabbed my ass. I did as I was told.

It had taken me two hours to get ready but the end result was flawless. My makeup was gorgeous and my hair was on point in a French roll and Chinese bang. My skin was oiled and smelled of Juicy Couture. I had chosen a red Christian Dior, spandex dress that fit like a glove all the way down to my ankles. The front of the dress dipped low in a V-cut that stopped just under my pierced navel. The back scooped off of my shoulders, exposing the cross that was tatted under my neck. My shoes were crystal covered Red Bottoms; they went so well with the jewelry from earlier.

I made my way down the off white spiraled staircase then headed into the dining room.
"Damn!" King and I said in unison. He was standing there looking fresh to death in his custom, black and burgundy, Christian Dior three piece suit.

He pulled my chair out then took the one to my left at the head of the table. "You look beautiful, Mrs. James."

"Thanks baby and you look debonair." I said filling my champagne flute with water.

"Tonight, I will be serving McDonalds." He lifted the brass lid that was covering my food. Sure as shit, there was an Angus burger and an order of fries. I cracked up laughing.

"What is this?"

"Well I wanted to show you that I haven't forgotten where we come from." King smiled and leaned in for a kiss. "Jazzy, I'm all about new things and different experiences but I never want to forget what made me who I am. You loved me when this was all I could afford and that means so much to me. I love having you in my life and I look forward to growing old with you." He raised his flute, "Here's to our future."

"Speaking of our future," I nervously raised my flute, "We're having another baby!" I clicked glasses with him and held my breath.

"Say what?" He scooted back from the table.

"I'm pregnant, King." I smiled but the look he gave me was deadly.

"See bitch, you just like the rest of them hoes out to get my money. A nigga blow up then y'all start poking holes in condoms and shit. What the fuck am I going to do with another baby, Jasmine?"

"King, I just thought it would be nice for Jordan to have someone to play with." I tried to keep an even tone but I was slowly registering what he had just said.

"Jordan is four and don't even know his own name, so how in the fuck is he going to play with some damn body!" His fists hit the marble table, causing me to flinch.

"Don't you talk about my son like that!" Now I was up and out of my seat. It was one thing to disrespect me but a whole different thing to disrespect my baby.

"What Jasmine? You know what I'm saying is true. Your son is a fuckin' retard and it's all your fault." King shook his head in disgust.

"How can you say that? Especially when he's your son too? Jordan is a person with feelings, not a retard. You treat him like shit and he feels it, it hurts! How in the hell could you talk about your only son that way?" I was boiling hot and had reached for the butter knife on the table before I realized it.

"Oh shit." He laughed. "You gon' stab me?"

"You better not let one more bad word about my son come from your mouth or I just might stab you!" My hand was trembling.

"As of tomorrow, your pregnant ass and *your* son need to find another place to stay! I got five kids already and I for damn sho don't need any more." He said it like he hadn't just dropped a bomb on me.

"Five kids? Who in the hell are the other four?" I felt weak and tried to hold myself up by holding on to the back of the chair.

"Don't act brand new! You knew I was fuckin' around. I got Prince, Princess, King Jr., and

Queenisha." He smiled, obviously proud of his offspring. "Shit, I got the whole royal family. All my kids are going to be something too."

I watched as he pulled a folded piece of aluminum foil from his back pocket. He opened it up and sniffed. No wonder he's wildin' out, his ass was getting high again. I bet D-Bo brought that shit to him earlier.

"How can you be so fuckin' evil? You're the devil; I should've left your ass a long time ago!" Although the tears were falling, I was numb to the pain.

"But you didn't, did you?" King removed his suit jacket. "Part of the reason that I stay with your dumb ass is because you take everything that I dish out." He laughed and I winced. I fuck hoes then come home to you with the juices on my dick from the next bitch and you still suck it because you ain't got no other choice!"

"Fuck you King!" I gripped the butter knife like it was a machete. "You better not come any closer." I was about to murder this nigga. Not only had he just confirmed his many affairs with multiple women, he had also admitted to having children, two of which belong to that bitch Tracey. "You ain't nothing but a piece of shit! I'm sorry that I ever loved you." I wiped my eyes.

"Yeah, yeah. That's what they all say." I heard him mumble as I ran upstairs.

Chapter Twenty-two
Lyric

Before I knew it, the Puerto Rico trip was here and I was ready to go. The kids were off to school and Damien had gone to the gym. Knowing his new movie was about to begin filming, Damien had been working out like a maniac. I was so happy to see him doing something productive with his time and mind. Finally, things were beginning to look better for my family and I was thrilled. Just as I closed the zipper on my carry-on, my cell phone rang. "Hello."

"Hey Lyric, it's Diamond. Are you busy?"

"Kind of but what's up?" I always wanted to make my clients feel like a priority even when I had a million things going on.

"Good. Girl, I need you to meet me on Rodeo Drive now. Ken is taking me to meet his family this week and I don't have anything mother approved in my closet." Diamond sounded worried.

"Right now?" Looking down at the watch on

my wrist, I only had three hours before I was set to leave for the airport with Tionne.

"It shouldn't take long. All I need are a few pieces for Alabama."

"Ok." I sighed, knowing damn well I was pushing it. However, I didn't want to decline Diamond's request when her boyfriend had me on retainer. "I'm leaving the house now. I'll meet you at Gucci.

After loading my bags into the trunk of my car, I headed out to meet her on Rodeo Drive. As soon as I started the engine, my phone started ringing again. This time, it was my mother. "Hey mama."

"Don't hey me. Why haven't you paid my car note?"

"Excuse me?" I didn't like the way she was talking to me.

"I said, why haven't you paid my car note? The repo man had the audacity to try to take my shit at the country club in front of everyone." My mother only cursed when she was angry.

"Mama, I heard you the first time. I only said excuse me for how you came at me." I paused, trying my best to remain respectful toward my mother. "I didn't pay your car note because I could barely pay mine!"

"Do you know I had to go in my purse and make a payment on the spot for them to take my car off the truck?" She continued as if I hadn't said a thing. "I had to give them five thousand dollars because of all the payments you missed."

"At least you had five thousand, got dammit!" I didn't mean to curse at my mother but she had taken me to a new level of irritation.

"Have you lost your mind, Lyric Lauren." She only used my middle name when I was in trouble. "Claud," she called for my father. "Your daughter done lost her mind. Pick up the phone."

"Hello." My father answered after fumbling with the second phone.

"Hey daddy."

"Hey pumpkin." My daddy proceeded to ask about Damien and the kids but was cut off as usual by my mother.

"Forget all the greetings. Tell your father what you had the nerve to say to me."

"Mom, the only reason I said that is because you don't listen. I've been telling you for a while now that things are not looking good over here. I've tried to tell you that I'm robbing Peter to pay Paul, barely able to pay my bills let alone yours too. I've tried telling you that I don't have any money but all you hear is what you want to hear. Instead of asking me if I'm okay and what you can do to help, all I hear you say is more, more, more." Without another word, I pressed the end button and hung up on my parents. By now, the tears were falling down my face. For so long, I hadn't been heard and it was beginning to wear me down. The entire family saw me as an ATM, ready and willing to dispense money at their request. I was tired of it all.

By the time I emerged from the car to meet Diamond, my tears had been replaced with a fresh coat of makeup; I was ready to do the job I'd been hired for. "Thanks for coming on short notice."

Diamond greeted me with a hug in front of the Gucci store.

"No problem." I embraced her back. "I only have three hours but I'll get you right in less than two." Holding the door open, we waltzed in like we owned the joint.

"I'm so nervous, Lyric. I really want his mom to like me." Diamond admitted while eying a navy blazer.

"Just be yourself. If she likes you, fine. If she doesn't, it's her loss. After all, you don't want her falling in love with someone you're not because then you'll have to keep up the façade forever."

"I never thought about it like that." Diamond nodded her head. "It's just that guys like Ken don't come around often and I don't want to lose him on account of his mother."

"I know what you mean but you can't worry about it. Ken loves you and that's all that matters." Immediately, I was drawn to a cream colored, casual, lounge ensemble with Gucci written in gold cursive letters. "I think you would look stunning in this on the airplane." I held it up to her.

"Um." The way her lips were twisted, I could tell this wasn't her taste. "What about this." She flew over to a pair of leopard skinny jeans and matching top. Gucci was written in red. It wasn't my thing but I wasn't the client.

"It could work, provided you have the right shoes."

"I like these." Diamond, grabbed the matching leopard boots off a display nearby.

"I think that's too much leopard." I shook my head. "How about you buy the top and the shoes then pair them with a black jean instead."

"I like that." She put the leopard pants back and we continued shopping.

Next, we stopped in bebe then Juicy. After grabbing several pieces, we ended the day at Neiman Marcus. Almost the entire time we shopped, I noticed a guy lurking not too far behind us. "Girl, I'm about to alert security."

"What's wrong?" Diamond looked up from the chair she was sitting in.

"Have you noticed this guy following us from store to store?" I pointed at the creep pretending to look at the ladies purse on display.

"Shit!" She stood abruptly, knocking over her bag in the process. "Give me a second." Diamond waltzed over to the guy and started going ham. I couldn't hear what she was saying but it was obvious the two of them knew each other. I tried not to stare, so I busied myself picking up the contents of her purse.

"What the fuck?" I frowned. On the floor were several blouses from the Gucci store with tags on them.

"Sorry Lyric, that was my old boyfriend." Diamond said before noticing her shit on the floor. "Why the fuck was you in my purse?" Quickly, she bent down and reloaded her bag with the hot goods.

"Girl, you knocked your bag over when you stood up. I was just picking your things up." I dropped one of the shirts and stood. "I'm out. I can't be associated with this." Grabbing my shit, I headed for the nearest exit.

"Lyric, wait up. Let me explain." Diamond was on my ass but I wasn't stopping. Just as we approached the front door, we were greeted by two police officers and an employee from the Gucci store. "That's them officer."

"Empty your bags!"

"Excuse me." Diamond snapped.

"Shit!" I couldn't believe this was really happening.

"Open up the bags or I will open them for you." One of the cops made a move for Diamond's purse and she hit him with it. Next thing I knew, all four of us were getting physical.

"Stop it!" I screamed. The male officers were forcefully pushing me and Diamond to the floor. "I didn't steal shit!"

"We saw the tape!" The store clerk yelled as both officer's slapped cuffs on me and Diamond. I watched as he went through my bag and then through Diamond's where all of her stolen items came tumbling to the floor.

"Let's take a ride to the station." I was lifted

to my feet.

"I didn't steal anything. I swear." I was practically crying now. Never had I been put in handcuffs and placed under arrest.

"Don't say shit, Lyric! I'ma call Ken. He'll handle it." Diamond yelled as she was escorted to one of the waiting squad cars and I was escorted to the other.

Chapter Twenty-three
Zuri

"Baby, I just wanted to stop by and give you a kiss before the car service comes to pick me up for the airport." I said after opening the door to Jason's office down the hall from our bedroom. He was sitting in the oversized chair on the phone. "Are you fucking sure!?" He barked, causing me to practically jump from my skin. Anytime he was on ten, I hated to be anywhere in the vicinity. "Fix this like I fucking pay you to do!" Jason slammed the phone down and leaped from his seat so fast I didn't have time to exit.

"What happened?" I asked while being backed into a corner.

"Trent Cambridge signed with Phillip! I can't believe this shit!" With his teeth gritted, Jason sent a body shot right to my side. "After all I did for that boy and he repays me by signing with my rival, making me lose out on a ten percent cut of thirty million dollars." Jason sent another blow to the same exact spot. This time, I dropped to the floor and balled up into the fetal position. "Get off the fucking floor. Your transportation will be here in a minute." Just like that, my husband stepped right over me then waltzed out the door.

For nearly fifteen minutes, I lay in the same spot too weak to stand and too scared to call out for help. It wasn't until Sylvia came in from her afternoon walk and yelled for me that I finally spoke. "I'm in here."

"Girl, I just met that fine ass neighbor of yours, Judge Pritchett. He may be y'all's new stepdaddy." She practically tripped over me in the doorway of the study. "Baby, what's the matter? Why are you on the floor?"

"Please just help me to the bathroom down the hall."

"Where is his black ass at?" She asked while carefully pulling me to my feet.

"I heard the front door close a few minutes before you came in. He probably went for a ride." I limped down the hall to the guest bathroom.

"Did he hurt you bad? Sit down on the toilet. Let me take a look."

"Ouch." I nearly jumped out of my skin as Sylvia tried to access the fresh bruises her son had applied to my rib cage.

"I think he may have broken something. You should see a doctor."

"I'll be fine." Taking ahold of the bathroom sink, I tried to pull myself up. It was hard to breathe and my shit ached with tremendous pain.

"What happened this time?" Sylvia assisted me to my feet.

"One of the guys Jason was scouting for his sports representation agency signed a deal with his competition." I sighed.

"Enough is enough! Next time he'll kill you." Sylvia was livid. "I didn't raise him like this Zuri." I could tell Syl was mortified by her son's actions.

"I know you didn't." I patted her hand before limping over to the master suite and scanning the vicinity for anything I forgot to pack. I'd had my moment to mope; now it was back to business as usual.

"When he comes home, I'll have a long talk with that boy. You don't deserve this, baby." Syl was more shaken up than I was.

"Don't worry about me, a few days on the beach and I'll be just fine." I tried to reassure my mother-in-law.

"Zuri, I really wish you would see a doctor." Syl grabbed my hand just as the doorbell chimed.

"I'll be fine." With a smile, I grabbed my purse and cell phone and tried my best to make it down the stairs. Truth was, I wasn't fine. Not only was my body in pain, my feelings were hurt. Although I pretended everything was ok, it wasn't. I was tired of being Jason's punching bag.

"Hey girl!" Tionne shouted from the foyer. The maid had let her in.

"Hey." I put on the biggest smile I cold muster. "Are you ready for Puerto Rico?"

"Hell yeah!" She started doing some dance that didn't have a name. "Where is Lyric?"

"I was just about to ask you the same thing. Wasn't she riding over with you?" With my hand gripping the stair rail for dear life, I made it down each one without revealing how much I was hurting.

"I've been calling her and her phone keeps going to voicemail." Tionne pulled out her phone and called Lyric once more. "See it went to voicemail again."

"I hope everything is ok."

"Me too." Tionne dialed again.

"I don't want to leave her but I don't want to waste first-class tickets." I laughed. "Let me text Leslie." Quickly, I shot a message to Lyric's daughter. Instantly, she texted back to let me know that her mom had a last minute client. I relayed the information to Tionne, so we decided to meet Lyric at the airport. There was no sense in all three of us missing our flights.

On the way out the door, Jason's car pulled back up. My stomach did a summersault as he stepped out but I remained cool. "Hey, Jay." Tionne nodded and he nodded back. I purposefully walked past him to the rear of the car where my daughter was sleeping peacefully. Not wanting to disturb her, I only blew a kiss in her direction then backed away. I was definitely going to miss Jelly but I needed space to think about my next move.

"Aren't you gon' say bye." Jason wrapped his massive arm around my waist, causing me to flinch.

"Ouch." I whispered. "That hurts."

"I love you with every fiber of my being. You know that right?" He whispered while releasing his embrace.

"I love you too." I replied. Both of our reflections were visible in the car mirror. I'm sure he saw when I rolled my eyes.

"Come on Z, let's roll." Tionne was turned all the way up.

"See you later." I pushed past my husband and made my way over to the waiting party bus ready to drop us off at the airport.

"Let's get the party started." Tionne was

already inside pouring the chilled champagne as I climbed the three short stairs to the bus in agony.

"Amen." I replied, although I was no longer in party mode. I couldn't help but feel uneasy about everything. For the first time in forever, I was questioning my love for Jason and my loyalty to our marriage. Sometime between this time and the last time he put his hands on me, my outlook about it had changed. I no longer wanted to be on the receiving end of his blows. Things needed to change and I was going to make sure of that the minute I returned home.

Chapter Twenty-four
Diamond

After spending nearly five hours down at the police station, they finally agreed to let us go with a warning. All I had to do was pay for my shirts and never return to the Gucci store again. "What the fuck is wrong with you?" Lyric was pissed. "Why are you stealing when there is a fucking black card in your wallet?"

"I don't want to talk about it." I said as we collected her shoes and personal items from the front desk.

"Fine, don't talk to me but Ken is gonna wanna know what your problem is right before he dumps your ghetto ass." She pointed to Ken on the other side of the door. He was casually resting on the bench in the waiting area beside Lyric's husband.

"Fuck!" I hadn't even thought about what I would say when he got here. The only reason I even dialed his number was because I knew he was the only person I could rely on to bail me out. Thinking fast, I pushed past Lyric and made my way into the lobby.

"Babe, are you alright?" Ken stood. "What happened?"

"It was awful." I started crying. "Ken, I've never been to jail a day in my life. I feel so ashamed and embarrassed."

"What happened? Was it a misunderstanding?" Ken wrapped his long arms around me.

"I called Lyric to go shopping with me for Alabama but I didn't know she was a thief."

"What!?" Lyric, Damien, and Ken all said concurrently.

"Bitch, I may be a lot of things but a thief ain't one of them." Lyric snapped. "Tell your man whose Birkin bag they pulled the Gucci tops from."

"Girl stop! You know you put that shit in my purse." I put my hand in her face. "My man gave me plenty of money to go shopping with. You're the only broke bitch around here. So it looks like you're the only one with a motive to steal."

"Ken, I know you don't believe that?" Lyric stepped to Ken.

"Lyric, I can't believe you would stoop to this level. We're done!"

"What?" She was flabbergasted. "Ken, are you serious? You know me."

"Listen, I can't be associated with this and neither can my girl. I don't know what you and your husband are into but we can't take part in that crazy shit." Ken looked down at Lyric.

"Fuck you nigga! Don't nobody talk to my wife like that." Damien jumped up but Lyric got in between them.

"Look Lyric, I need my money back. If you can't afford to return it in full by Friday, then you might as well find a legal aid attorney because I will be taking you to court." Ken grabbed my hand and pulled me toward the door. I wanted to laugh at how Lyric was about to cry, it was pathetic.

"Baby, please get me out of here." With my head down, I flew to Ken's car parked curbside.

Once inside, I continued to make up a colorful story about Lyric and her "thieving" ass. Ken felt bad that he had introduced me to such a character and apologized profusely. "I just hope they don't publish the story and your mother sees it along with my mugshot."

"Don't worry baby, we'll explain everything if necessary." Ken patted my knee. With a smirk, I reclined in the seat and retrieved my cell phone from my bag. During the time I'd been in the holding cell, I'd missed ten calls. Most of the numbers were unfamiliar, so I checked the messages.

"Bitch, when I see you, I'ma kill you and your boyfriend! You can run but you can't hide. I got eyes everywhere!" I didn't recognize the voice but I knew it had to be Omar. I had no idea why he was mad but the next message was from my brother. Hopefully, he would give me some insight.

"Diamond, what the fuck man! I vouched for you. Call me back."

"What is going on?" I mumbled to myself.

Ken was so busy blasting his music that he wasn't paying me any mind. It's a good thing too because as soon as the third voicemail started playing and I heard Grace's voice, my whole face hit the floor.

"Diamond, it's Grace. You know it's hard to believe me and you were once like sisters. I let you into my home and you stole my shit?" Grace laughed. "Although I could give less than a fuck about your skank ass, I thought you should know all of those vials were filled with small pieces of chipped soap, not heroin. You won't get a dollar from that package, you bum bitch!"

It was all starting to make sense now and my stomach was in a knot. My life was officially in danger and I had no one to blame but myself. Omar was surely going to kill me for selling him fifteen thousand dollars worth of chipped soap. As much as I loved Ken, it was time to do what I did best; hop on a plane and get ghost.

"Duck!" Ken screamed.

"Huh?" Instantly, I looked up expecting to find the piece of shit skeleton from my closet.

Instead, what I found was a blue Chevy riding extremely close. The driver of the vehicle held a large caliber weapon out of the window and started blasting. BLAH. BLAH. BLAH. The car was riddled with bullets. I could tell Ken was hit by the way he slumped over on me. Desperately, I tried to take hold of the steering wheel but it was too late. We sped into an embankment and became airborne.

Chapter Twenty-five
Tionne

The entire ride to the airport was silent. Something was up with Zuri and I knew it. "Hey girl, are you alright?"

"Yeah, I'm good just thinking about life you know." Zuri gulped down her drink and continued staring out of the window.

"What's wrong, Z. Talk to me." It was unlike her to be so detached. Every time we were together, it was a party but today seemed more like a funeral.

"Everything is wrong Tionne but you wouldn't understand."

"Me not understand?" I felt offended. "Don't you know what I've been going through lately? My husband is a cheater, and I don't have any money. I think I may be a little more understanding than you think." I said before smacking my lips.

"It's not like that, T."

"Well what is it like then? We're best friends. You should be able to talk to me about anything. I talk you to about everything." I was becoming frustrated.

"Tionne, no offense, but you tell me all of your business because you want to. Some things are private to me and this is one of them." Zuri was getting irritated.

"Whatever Zuri, I see how it is." With my arms crossed, I pulled out my phone and checked Instagram. "You know sometimes, I think you believe you're better than me." By now, the champagne was talking.

"Girl bye." Zuri dismissed me with the wave of her hand.

"It's the truth." I retorted. "You have the perfect life with a perfect career, a perfect child, and perfect husband who gives you money and takes you on trips to places most people can't even pronounce. All of the stars aligned when you fell from between your mother's legs." I giggled. "Miss fucking perfect."

"Really Tionne, we're gonna go there?" Zuri stood from her seat. "Well tell me Tionne, does living in a perfect world include getting my ass beat every got damn time my perfect husband has a bad day?" With tears, Zuri lifted her shirt to not only show me the fresh bruises on her side, but the old wounds on her back.

"Z, I'm sorry." I was completed floored.

"Forgive me if I'm not so quick to tell you that my nose has been broken, my shoulder has been dislocated, or that my teeth have been knocked out. It's not exactly a got damn conversation starter." Zuri wiped her face with the back of her hand.

"Please forgive me. I had no idea. Please forgive me." I stood and hugged my friend who was crying hysterically. She sounded like a child as she gagged on her tears.

"I'm scared." Zuri sniffed. "One day, he will kill me, Tionne. What about Jelly?"

"No, he won't. I swear because we're going to get you out of there." Now I was crying too.

"We're going to turn this bus around and go home and get your shit."

"Jason won't let that happen." Zuri broke our embrace.

"We'll call the police if need be."

"No, I don't want him to get in any trouble." Zuri shook her head profusely.

"Fuck him!" I spat. "I say we roll up in that bitch with Five O, grab Jelly and your things, and get ghost." The Detroit in me was emerging. As the saying goes, you can take the girl out of the hood but you can't take the hood out of the girl.

"It's not that simple. If I do this the wrong way, Jason will make me pay severely for it."

"We can get you a restraining order, Z."

"Girl bye, what is a piece of paper going to do to protect me?" Zuri looked at me sideways. "You know the type of pull being a celebrity has."

"You're right." I sighed, taking the seat beside her. Oftentimes, having star status put you above the law for a little hush money and an autograph.

"I need a plan, Tionne." Zuri rested her head in her lap.

"How about we cancel this girl's trip and go back to my hotel room to regroup." Wrapping my arms around Zuri, I squeezed her tightly. I could only imagine what my friend had been enduring in the name of love. She was a good person who deserved much better. I felt guilty for thinking her life was a fairytale when in reality she was trapped in a nightmare.

"That's actually a good idea." Zuri popped her head up. "Jason has a big conference downtown tomorrow that should last about four hours. I can use that time to get my shit and get out before he comes back."

"Let's do the damn thing." I extended my hand.

"You don't have to go, Tionne. I don't want to drag you into my mess." Zuri shook her head.

"Bitch, me and you are down like four flats on a Cadillac!" There was no way I would send her into the lion's den alone. Jason couldn't whip both of us at the same time. Therefore, I was prepared for war.

Chapter Twenty-six
Jasmine

I laid awake in the guest suite down the hall from my bedroom all last night, replaying every single word exchanged between me and my husband. Not only had I come to the conclusion that King really probably never loved me. I also reached the revelation that I was a joke to my best friend. Her nephew and niece were my muthafuckin' step kids. That bitch Stacey had to know King was fucking around on me with her sister. For God's sake, Prince is four years older than Jordan and Princess is six months younger.

My mind raced as I reminisced about the times we went on shopping trips or girl's weekends out-of-town. She was keeping my ass busy while her sister was probably over here playing house up in my shit! "That dirty trick!" I said aloud as it finally hit me. The reason Tracey's ass is mini ballin' is because of King. My husband was the one footing her bills. He was either breaking her off or paying child support. That's how that heffa went and spent six stacks the other day. "If I wanted King, I could've had him." Her words echoed in my head. "Your gold-diggin' ass won't want him when I'm done." I said out loud to myself and laughed wickedly. I was about to make this muthafucka pay for all the years that I'd been living in hell.

After sliding on a black spaghetti strapped, tank top and pulling on my black Juicy Couture bottoms with the gold lettering, I slipped on my gold metallic, UGG boots and was out of the room in no time. I walked down the stairs and toward the voices coming from the study. "What time are we leaving for the airport?" I poked my head inside the door. Both King and D-Bo stared as if they had seen a ghost.

"Um, we?" King looked confused.

"Yeah, we. I want to ride with you to the airport, since I won't be seeing you for a few days." I smiled and he frowned.

"Yo D-Bo, let me holler at Jasmine right quick big dog." He leaned back in the oversized, leather, swivel chair.

"No problem boss. I'll be outside." D-Bo walked his 311 pounds lightly past me like his ass was walking on egg shells. "Morning Jasmine."

"D-Bo," was all I gave him along with a slight nod. I walked into the warm, neutral colored space then pulled the French doors closed.

"Are you okay?" King scratched his forehead.

"Couldn't be better?" I smiled, flashing all of my pearly whites. "How are you this morning?"

"I'm good." He cleared his throat. "Look Jazzy, about last night I..."

I cut him off, "What about last night?" I waved my hand, "It's old news right? I mean you did say everything you needed to say didn't you?"

"Um, yeah I guess, but..."

"But nothing, it's water under the bridge. Now what time is that flight?"

"I actually need to be leaving now." King stood from the chair in his navy blue Sean John sweat suit.

"Well let's hit the road; we don't want you to miss it." Quickly, I spun around and proceeded to the front door. The minute this asshole was in the sky, I was coming back here and cleaning him out.

Minutes later, we were on our way. "Damn D-Bo, slow down before we get pulled over." King called from the backseat. I must admit D-Bo was pushing it but the quicker we got King to the airport, the happier I would be.

"Boss, you only got twenty minutes before the plane leaves. We need to get there!" He insisted.

"Arrive Alive! Ain't you ever heard that saying?" King reached up and held onto the handle we used for hanging our dry cleaning up.

"We're almost there boss." We bent a few more corners, flew over a pot hole or two, and blew a red light right in front of a cop.

"Damn!" I was the one that spoke up this time. Just as I feared, lights began to flash and the sirens blared.

"Nigga, if I miss this flight, that's your job." King threatened. D-Bo pulled over just as the officer had instructed over the speaker. Slowly coming to a stop with the police officer on our bumper, we sat there in silence. "Jazz, let me see your purse." King spoke as the officer stepped from the vehicle marked Sheriff.

"Why?" I asked.

"I need to put my phone in there."

"Why?" I asked again.

"Because," he clinched his teeth. "These officers fuck with me after they recognize who I am. The last time I was pulled over, they searched the car and took my phone."

"What's so special about your phone?" I was still confused.

"It ain't about the phone; it's about what's in it. You know how many other celebrity's numbers and addresses I got in my phone. I got a lock on it but nowadays people can hack into everything."

Not thinking twice about it, I handed over my Dooney & Burke seconds before the officer tapped on the door.

"License, insurance, and registration sir." He

asked while looking back at us. D-Bo handed over the items. Then the older, African American officer reviewed them thoroughly. "Son, do you know why I pulled you over?"

"'Cause I'm black?" D-Bo responded with much attitude. Was his big ass blind? The officer was as black as midnight his damn self.

"Don't get cute with me, son."

"I ain't your son." D-Bo added. I was about to pass out in the backseat. *No he didn't just say what I thought he said.*

"What's with the attitude and why did you run that red light?" The officer asked.

"I'm trying to get my boss to the airport and I don't got no attitude."

"You realize you could've killed someone back there?" The officer removed his sunglasses.

"Wasn't nobody coming when I blew that light and you know it." D-Bo was working my nerve and by the looks of it, King's too.

"Officer, I apologize for my driver's behavior. Today is his first day and I think he's a lil nervous." King rolled his window down and lied with a straight face.

"Hey, aren't you that fella from the television?" The officer peered at King.

"Yes sir! My name is King James but you may know me as KJ." King extended his hand which the officer shook it.

"Yeah KJ, my grandkids watch your videos all the time. I've seen one or two myself and I want you to know that they sicken me," he frowned.

"Excuse me?" King said.

"All you talk about is sex and drugs. It's very distasteful son. You disrespect our women and teach our children that it's ok to sell and use drugs." He shook his head.

"Old man, are you done talking? We got places to be." D-Bo chimed in, causing me to roll my eyes. He had struck a nerve with the officer.

"Everybody step from the vehicle; now!" Right after, he drew his weapon. We jumped from the car with our hands up. "Have a seat over there on the sidewalk. If one of you moves, you're all going to jail.

My heart damn near jumped from my chest as he searched D-Bo's Trailblazer. I didn't know what he was liable to find on the inside of that thing but I was silently praying that it was nothing that would land us in jail. No one made a sound as the officer headed back over to us. I didn't know if it was me but he seemed to be going in slow motion as he carried my purse. "Ma'am, could you step over here for a second."

On wobbly legs, I took five long steps toward him, "Yes sir?"

"This is your bag, correct?" He held it up and I nodded.

"Yes sir, that's my purse." I felt a lump form in my throat.

"Please turn around for me and place your hands behind your back. You're under arrest!" He said with force although his face read disappointment.

"Why am I being arrested?" I asked over my shoulder. He secured the cuffs then turned me around to face him.

"You're being arrested for the possession of narcotics. Does this look familiar?" He waved a sandwich bag in front of my face. It looked like baby powder and reminded me of what King was sniffing last night.

"That's not mine officer!" I screamed.

"Possession is nine-tenths of the law, baby." King called from the sidewalk with his cell phone glued to his ear. The same cell phone that he had asked to put in my purse. I had been set-up by my own fuckin' husband.

After the officer read me my rights, I was placed in the back of the squad car. I looked on as he handed D-Bo a ticket along with his other documentation. "Jasmine, I'll be back in two days okay; just hang tight baby." With that said, I watched as my husband threw me the deuces and pulled off to go shoot his music video in Atlanta. I shook my head in disbelief. This nigga had just left me on stuck with a damn possession charge.

"Ma'am, can I call anyone for you?" The

officer asked. "Sometimes you're not given a phone call until they finish booking you and processing your information. It could be hours and you look like a nice girl. I would hate for you to have to wait that long." The officer explained.

"Thank you sir, can you call my mother?" I rattled off the number to her home phone. When she didn't pickup, I gave the officer her cell number, but she didn't answer that either.

"Maybe your boyfriend will get ahold of her." He made eye contact with me through the rearview mirror.

"That's my husband, and I doubt it." I mumbled.

"That guy is your husband?" He became wide-eyed. "And he just left you like this?" He said while shaking his head. "You young people never cease to amaze me." He chuckled while I frowned.

"Look, I was leaving him today. As soon as he got on the plane, I was packing up me and my son and we were out." I didn't know why but I felt as if I had to explain myself.

"Is that right?"

I could tell by his tone that he didn't believe me for one second, but I was dead serious.

As we pulled into the police station which was about two miles from the airport, my stomach began to ache. I wasn't sure if it was the baby, hunger pains, or the fact that I was nervous as hell. Aside from watching the show *Cops* on TV, I have never been up close and personal with the law. The officer came around to open my door and help me out of the car. I looked at his name tag which read Sheriff Johnson. "Okay, this is it; we're here."

The place resembled a small office and was a little too spiffy to be for the bad guys. The waiting area looked cozy and smelled of fresh paint. The linoleum floors were waxed and shining. There was also a fresh smell in the air. I was pleased that since I had to be taken to jail at least it was this one. "What's going on Frank?" The female officer behind the receptionist desk asked after looking up from her Sloppy Gossip magazine.

"Nothing much Lizzie. This is Mrs. Jasmine

James; she's being charged for the possession of cocaine." Frank leaned on the counter as I cringed at what he had just said. Officer Lizzie glanced up at me then back down at her magazine.

"Are you King James's wife?" She looked bewildered. I started to say no but maybe saying yes would work in my favor. Officer Johnson was old school and by the book. Perhaps, this thirty-something year old lady would let me pass for an autograph, picture, free CD, or something.

"Yes. That's me." I stood tall, flung my hair over my shoulder, and tried to appear as glamorous as she probably thought I was.

"Wow! This is not your week, huh?" She turned her magazine toward me. You could have bought me for a penny right then and there; I was too done. Right there, smack dab in the middle of the page was a picture of me on the floor being pulled by King. My mouth was wide open, my makeup was a mess, and there was a huge, red star covering my exposed private part. The title of the article was "Young & Reckless."

"Not my week at all." I was too ashamed to look her in the face, so I looked down at the floor instead.

Right after the humiliating moment, I was handed over to Officer Lizzie and taken to the back for booking. "Hold this sign and look straight ahead. Turn left, now turn right." She instructed. I knew my mug shots would hit the Internet by tomorrow, so I tried my best to look fabulous. After the photo shoot, I was finger printed, drug tested, and allowed my phone call. "Praise the Lord and leave a message. BEEP." My mother's voicemail came on and I rolled my eyes. *Where was she when I needed her?* I thought to myself.

"Hey mama, it's me. I got into some trouble and I need you to bail me out." I rattled off the address and phone number to the precinct before hanging up the beige desk phone.

"Would you like to call King?" Lizzie asked like she knew him and we were cool like that.

"He's out-of-town." I sighed.

"What about a lawyer? Rich people keep

those on standby." She commented.

"The only lawyer we have is an
entertainment lawyer and she's out of Georgia." I
explained. Truth-be-told, even if the bitch was
around the corner, I didn't have a number to reach
her at. She was King's attorney and I had only met
her once at a fundraiser.

"What about friends?"

I looked at her and almost broke into tears as
I thought about Stacey. Other than my mother, she
was the only person in my life I knew for sure had
my back. Up until last night, I thought she was my
one, true-blue friend. Boy was I wrong!

"Nope, no friends either." I replied.

"Okay, well maybe your mom will get the
message and call you back." Lizzie almost looked
sorry for me.

We walked down a short hallway and
stopped in front of a door marked HOLDING.
"Can't I just post my own bail?" I asked,
remembering hearing something like that on one of
my TV shows. I needed to get the hell out of here

and fast. I only had two days to work with before King was back. By the looks of it, I'll be here for at least a few more hours.

"You won't be given a bond until tomorrow morning. You'll go before the judge and he'll set it then." Lizzie unlocked the white door.

"Tomorrow?" I repeated and she nodded. Losing a day would really put a damper on my plans but I was determined to leave King and pay those no good twins a lesson before Jordan, my mom, and I left town. I needed a fresh start and a new beginning.

Chapter Twenty-seven
Diamond

All night I had tossed and turned on the chair in the hospital lobby and awoke with a stiff neck. Ken had been rushed to surgery with several gunshot wounds to various parts of his body. Miraculously, I only sustained minor cuts and bruising. One of the bullets had pierced my arm but other than a few stitches, I was fine. "Miss, were you the one in the car with Mr. Tucker?" One of the two men who approached me asked. Right off the bat, I knew they were detectives. Surprisingly, they hadn't showed up to question me yesterday when it all happened. However, I knew it was coming sooner or later.

"Yes, my name is Diamond. Ken is my fiancée. Is he okay?" The hospital hadn't relinquished any information to me yet because I wasn't immediate family.

"Unfortunately, we're unable to give up details at this time." The officer patted my shoulder before taking a seat beside me. His partner continued standing with notepad and pen in hand.

"I am his fucking fiancé; I deserve to know if he's dead or alive!"

"Calm down Ms. Diamond, I didn't mean to upset you. Off the record, Mr. Tucker is alive." The officer extended his card. "My name is Officer Kemp and this is Officer Brown. We were assigned to your fiancée's case. Can you recount yesterday for me?"

"I already told the cops on the scene I didn't see shit." I rolled my eyes.

"Ms. Diamond, I didn't ask you what you saw; I simply asked you to recount the day's events." Officer Kemp calmly chewed on a piece of gum while staring me down. This wasn't his first rodeo but it wasn't mine either.

"Ken had just picked me up and we were heading home. I was looking at my phone when the car went airborne. I thought we had been in a car accident until the paramedics said otherwise."

"What happened between the time of the

crash until the paramedics arrived?" Officer Brown asked.

"I don't know, I was unconscious after hitting my head on the dashboard." Quickly, I pointed to my dome. There was a small, three-inch cut from a shard of glass on my forehead but they didn't know that so I went with it. Truth is, I was alert and very much conscious after the car finally landed on the roof. I even almost pissed on myself as one of Omar's goons approached our car to finish the job. He would have succeeded if it wasn't for the fact that people were pulling over to offer help. Once he heard sirens, he disappeared.

"Do you know why someone would shoot at your fiancée's car?" Brown continued.

"No I don't. Ken is well-loved." I shook my head.

"Maybe he wasn't the one with enemies." Officer Kemp didn't bat an eyelash.

"What are you implying? Now I was being defensive.

"A pretty little girl with a past meets the

next Jordan and gets him to fall in love with her could warrant plenty of enemies, wouldn't you say?"

"Sounds logical to me." Brown added.

"Maybe one of your friends from the hood became jealous." Officer Kemp continued. I was about to dog-check his ass but that's when Ken's mother came through the lobby causing a scene.

"Is my baby okay?" She bum-rushed the front desk.

"I'm sorry. Who is your baby?" The receptionist asked.

"Ken Joseph Tucker."

"Excuse me, gentlemen. I need to speak with my mother-in-law." I stood without another word then headed over to the small crowd of people behind her.

"May I go and see him please?" Mrs. Tucker begged.

"Your son was in surgery all night ma'am. As soon as he leaves the recovery area for his room in the intensive care unit, we will send you right up." The receptionist smiled. "Have a seat right there and I'll come and get you as soon as Mr. Tucker is ready for visitors."

"Thank you." Mrs. Tucker and her family took a seat near the front desk and I joined them.

"Excuse me Mrs. Tucker; my name is Diamond. Ken is my boyfriend." I spoke softly. At first, she looked at me like she could care less but then she smiled.

"How are you holding up Diamond?"

"I'm okay, just a little shaken up." I took the seat across from her.

"This is your fault!" A voice came from behind me. I looked up to see Ken's sister; I recognized her from a photo on his wall. Ken told me she was in the police academy. "My brother is a good boy. He's never done anything to anyone! You brought this trouble didn't you?"

"Excuse me?" I was appalled.

"Bitch! My fucking brother is a multimillionaire. You better believe I do my research on any and everybody he comes in contact with."

"You got me twisted." I stood to prepare myself in case she started swinging.

"Diamond, my brother may not have known he was trying to wife a stripper but I planned on telling him at mama's birthday party."

"What does my past have to do with Ken loving me?" I challenged her.

"It has a lot to do with it when you're known for coning men for money." The sister whose name I couldn't remember barked back. I'm not going to lie, that one stung a lot. It was a grim reminder that I was who I was no matter how much I wanted to change.

"Diamond, I think it would be best for you to leave." Mrs. Tucker stood.

"I can't leave without Ken knowing I'm here." I felt so hurt. Ken was the first man I loved in a very long time. It killed me to know his family was denying me access in his time of need.

"Bullshit!" The sister hollered.

"I'll make sure he knows." Mrs. Tucker took

her seat and waited patiently for me to go. With my head lowered, I nodded and walked away. I knew if Ken's family kicked me out of the hospital, they would have no problem kicking me out of his house. I had no where to go but I did have his blank check in my purse from the other day. I could use it to buy myself a new life and new identity. By the time he got out of the hospital and realized what I had done, I'd be long gone, never to be seen or heard from again.

Fuck Ken, Fuck California, Fuck Omar and Duck. It was time for me to get the fuck out of dodge. I no longer gave a shit about who I owed. I was tired of looking over my shoulder. With Ken's money, I would be set for the rest of my life; no longer selling myself to men for money. Anticipation and dollar signs had me dancing while rummaging through Ken's belongings. I was sure he had a hidden stash somewhere around here and my greed wouldn't let me leave without it. However, when I heard the front door open, that's when I realized I had stayed a minute too long.

Quietly, I headed to the hallway and peered over the banister. That's when I saw two gunmen searching the downstairs. Their mouths were covered with blue bandanas, the same as the one the shooter wore yesterday. Therefore, I knew Omar had sent them. Slowly, I backed away and ran back into Ken's bedroom. Subsequent to grabbing my purse, I headed over to the balcony and used it to escape. The drop was only one story, so I jumped it with ease. As soon as my feet hit the dirt, I flew back toward the front of the condo like a track star.

After checking to assure the coast was clear, I sprinted toward my car then jumped in. Pulling off on two wheels, I'm sure I left skid marks. "Hell yeah!" I hit the steering wheel with excitement, completely finding it unbelievable that I had managed to get away with my life and the money.

I drove for nearly thirty minutes across town to the bank branch I used to frequent with Ken. Even though I wasn't on his account, I'd gone with him so many times that I had a rapport with a few of the staff. After pulling into the parking lot, I killed the engine and pulled the folded check from my purse. Nervously, I stared at the paper before pulling out a pen and completing the document, signature and all. Forgery was something I learned back in school. My grades weren't too good which meant I went home with a lot of papers for my mother to sign. When I got tired of punishments and ass whippings, I learned how to write her name perfectly. Over time, I learned other people's as well. Ken's was one of them and it was relatively easy. It was the first letter in his first and last name then one squiggly line following each one. "Now you ain't trying to ditch me without repaying your debt are you?" Duck's voice startled me. He'd been laying on the floor for the entire ride.

"Shit!" I hollered before looking into the rearview mirror. Duck had a gun pointed at the back of my seat. "I wasn't trying to ditch no one. I got your money right here." I waved the check. "I just need to go in there and cash it."

"I'm going with you."

"You can't. I've never gone in there with

anyone besides Ken. If I show up with you and a large check payable to me, they will know something is up." I couldn't believe I'd been so close to walking away Scot-free. Duck showing up wasn't going to stop my plan though.

"Fine. I'll wait here but don't take long." He nodded for me to get out and that's exactly what I did.

With my head held high and strutting like a peacock, I swung the door open to First National and approached the teller. "Hey Diamond, where's the big guy?" Lula, my favorite of all the tellers asked.

"I don't know if you heard but we had a pretty bad accident yesterday." I pointed to my head. "Ken had to have surgery; he'll be down for a while."

"Oh my goodness. I'm sorry to hear that. This is news to me." Lula shook her head. "Is he alright though?"

"It's pretty bad." I nodded before producing the check and laying it on the counter. "His family has come up from Alabama and taken over. They even had the nerve to kick me out of the hospital. Can you believe that?"

"I know how it is. The same thing happened to my sister when her boyfriend of fifteen years died in a plane crash. The family put her out of his house, told her she couldn't help plan the funeral, and to not even show up at the services." Lula paused before picking up the check then fixating on it.

"Ken didn't want me to be without while he went through this fight for his life, so he gave me a little something to hold me down because he knew his mother wouldn't." I tried to look depressed for dramatic affect.

"Diamond, this is a lot of money. I have to speak with my manager first. Have a seat and I'll be back, okay." Lula smiled and backed away. Just as I went to take a seat on the sofa, she was back. "He said it's a go. Give me time to get it ready then you'll be good to go."

"Really?" I caught myself and cleaned it up.

"Good, I thought I would in here all day." Feeling a little more confident, I grabbed a magazine, sat back, and crossed my legs.

During the entire forty minutes I waited, I couldn't stop the smile from displaying on my face. The thought of being a millionaire had me tickled pink. I was so caught up in my thoughts that I was oblivious to those around me. Life was about to change and I couldn't wait. "She's right there." I heard Lula say then I looked up to see who she was talking to.

"Diamond Herrington, please stand. You're under arrest for grand larceny."

Chapter Twenty-eight
Jasmine

"Jasmine James, on the charge of possession, how do you plead?" The white, heavyset judge asked me the next day. I pondered my answer for a quick second. *That shit was not mine; hell, I didn't even know it was in my purse, your honor.* I thought about saying what was on my mind. Instead, one word tumbled out. "Guilty."

"Typically, in a case like this, I recommend twelve to eighteen months of jail time or a mandatory six month stay at a drug rehabilitation center for addicts in need of recovery." He removed his glasses and I swallowed hard because I couldn't do either jail or rehab.

"However Mrs. James, because this is your first offense, and your urine samples from the lab were clean," Judge J.D. Waters spoke through the closed circuit television. "I'm letting you off with a fine of fifteen hundred dollars, and a warning to never be caught in this situation again!

Understood?"

"Yes sir, your honor sir!" I practically shouted.

"We will enter your plea of guilty and your release agreement into the system. Your court fees are an additional two hundred dollars. Your release will be granted once payment in full for bail and court fees have been obtained. Court adjourned!"

I was so happy that I could've kissed him. In a mater of an hour, I was a free woman. My mother still had not answered her phone and I was worried to death. Lizzie handed me my purse and cell phone which Officer Johnson had confiscated yesterday. The minute I powered my cell up, text messages and voicemails came left and right. The first few messages were from Stacey, so I deleted them ASAP. The last few were from my mom. The hairs on the back of my neck stood up. "Hey baby, it's mama," sniffle. "Call me when you get this; I'm at Michigan Valley Hospital," sniffle. "Just get here when you can baby, okay. My phone is going to die, just get here." She repeated. My heart raced; I knew something wasn't right. I called a cab and within minutes, I was on my way to the hospital. I tried my mom again but no answer. Next, I called King.

"You out?"

"Surprised?" I snapped.

"What up; whatchu want?" He asked with a little irritation.

"Have you spoken to my mother? She called from Michigan Valley, crying and upset."

"She was blowing my phone up like crazy yesterday. I didn't answer 'cause I was busy and I thought it was about you being locked up." He admitted.

"I hope everything is okay with Jordan." Panic was evident in my voice.

"That lil nigga alright. Stop worrying and call me back later, they waiting for me to shoot this next part." King hung up before I had the chance to say bye or anything else for that matter.

Placing my phone back inside my purse, I closed my eyes and prayed that everything was okay. Maybe Jordan had a cold or something. My mother was more overprotective than me when it came to him. She probably noticed something small like a runny nose or slight cough and took him to see a doctor.

"Thirty-five dollars." The Arab driver pulled in front of the hospital. I pulled out two twenties, slid them through the mini-door, and told him to keep the change. I walked through the revolving door of the hospital then marched right up to the receptionist.

"Hi, I'm looking for Jordan James or Wanda Foster?" I gave both names because I wasn't sure if the patient was Jordan or my mother. The dark-skinned clerk with the finger-waved eighties hair-do typed vigorously. I scanned the waiting area in search of my mother while I waited.

"Oh," she looked up in horror. "Give me one second, I'll have someone come and get you." She lifted a red painted index finger, indicating one moment. I rolled my eyes and sighed loudly. The anxiety was about to kill me but I didn't want to take my frustrations out on her, so I walked away. I was pacing back and fourth for approximately ten minutes before a guy in green scrubs and a white lab coat approached me.

"Please ma'am, follow me." He said then turned away. I was hot on his trail. I thought it was odd that he didn't greet me like a normal doctor but I was just trying to get to my family so I didn't say anything. We stepped on the elevator in silence. I watched as he pressed the ground button, causing me to raise an eyebrow. Never had I been taken to the basement of a hospital. Thus, I wondered just what in the hell was going.

"What's down here?"

"Your mother is down here waiting for you." He replied without looking at me. The elevator buzzed then we stepped off. "Right this way." The man nodded and we turned left. I held my breath as we walked past an office door, an employee break room, and a large door marked Trash. Just as I was about to ask him where we were going again, my mother ran over to me with her arms wide open.

Chapter Twenty-nine
Lyric

After leaving the police station yesterday, it seemed that my streak of bad luck had returned. Not only did Ken want all the money I'd already spent but then Damien received a call on the way home advising us that his movie didn't get the proper financing it needed. Therefore, they were cancelling production. Furthermore, after my mugshot for shoplifting made its way online, the media had a field day with the story. Before I knew it, my phone was blowing up with clients either demanding an explanation or wanting to drop me all together. To top things off, I'd missed my flight to Puerto Rico.

"Do you want something to eat? I'm taking the kids out for burgers." Damien poked his head inside the bedroom. With all the shades pulled, the room was completely black. I was buried beneath the covers with the pillow over my face.

"We don't have money for burgers." I reminded him.

"Lyric, we'll figure this out."

"We need to sell the house before the bank takes it." My mind was on autopilot. All I could think of was where to go from here. "I'm calling the car company too. They can have their shit as well."

"Let's not be so extreme, baby." Damien stepped further into the room.

"I'm not being extreme. I'm being realistic." I sat up. "Fuck it all. Fuck everybody. I'm tired of pretending. I'm tired of it all." I rambled.

"Lyric, you're not the losing kind. Don't let one battle bring you down." Damien rested a hand on my shoulder.

"I'm tired of fighting a battle I'm never going to win."

"Daddy, come on." Leslie called from the hallway.

"Let's finish this when I get back, okay." Damien kissed my lips softly and I felt a tear slide down my check.

"Love you Damien. Tell the kids I love them too." I blurted out as he closed the bedroom door.

My husband was right; I wasn't a loser. Lyric Nicole Robertson always had a game plan for my family even if it meant sacrificing myself in the process. "The insurance policy!" I sprung from the bed, went to the safe in the closet, and retrieved the folder marked *IMPORTANT.* It contained birth certificates, social security cards, and our insurance policies. Quickly, I scanned through the pages and smiled. If something were to happen to me, my children would receive one million dollars each to be dispensed in two hundred thousand dollar increments at ages eighteen, twenty-one, twenty-five, thirty, and thirty-five. Damien would receive his million in increments every two years, provided he passed random drug tests setup by my attorney. The policy was something I put in place after Damien's first drug debacle. Now I was happy that I had always managed to make my annual payments.

Staring at the document and knowing what I was about to do, reality hit me hard. Nonetheless, I was determined not to change my mind. Heading over to the bathroom, I grabbed some pain meds from the time I broke my leg last year at Leslie's skating party. The bottle was nearly full of Percocet when I tipped it back and began swallowing. Reaching for the glass on the counter I gargled with in the morning, I filled it with water and continued digesting the pills. Before they kicked in, I took one last look in the mirror then went to lie down in bed. I didn't want to write any letters because I didn't want my children to remember me by final words. I didn't want to make any calls either because I didn't want anyone to stop me. All I wanted was peace and to be free of my burdens.

Closing my eyes, I calmly breathed in and out, trying to relax my mind. Rather quickly, I began to hallucinate then my breathing became slower and shorter. It felt as if someone was holding a pillow over my face and I began to burn up. I tried to raise my arms to lift the imaginary pillow but my body wouldn't move. Blinking hastily, I tried hard to focus. No longer did I like this feeling. I needed to grab the phone and call for help. "I don't want to die." I mumbled as my heart started racing. "Help me!"

"Lyric, what did you do? Oh my God! Leslie, call 911." I could hear Damien and my children screaming, but it was too late. Within an instant, everything went dark. It was lights out for Lyric Nicole Richardson.

Chapter Thirty
Jasmine

"Hey mama, are you okay?" I asked because she was visibly upset and shaken by something.

"Oh baby, my beautiful baby." She dabbed at her eyes with a crumbled piece of Kleenex.

"What's wrong mama? Where's Jordan?" I strained my neck to look over her shoulder.

"Come and sit down with me baby." She pulled me toward a set of chairs leaning against the stale, yellow wall.

"Mama, you're really scaring me right now. Where is my baby?" I had started to cry and I hadn't even received any news yet. I could tell by the feeling deep in the pit of my stomach that something was wrong, just like the day Jordan was born. My mother patted my back then looked up toward the Heavens.

"Baby, Jordan has gone on to be with the Lord in His Kingdom." She said, but it didn't quite register with me.

"Jordan went where...and to be with who?"
I questioned.

"Jasmine, Jordan has gone on to glory baby.
Mama wants you to be strong okay." She held me as
I collapsed into her arms.

"Are you saying my child is dead!?" I
screamed and she nodded with a tear stained face.
"When did this happen, mama?" Closing my eyes, I
pulled on my hair.

"Yesterday afternoon I went to wake him up
from his nap for lunch and he was gone. The Lord
took him in his sleep, Jasmine. I'm so sorry baby;
I'm so very sorry." My mother sniffled. "I tried to
reach you and King but I couldn't get either of
you."

"You've been here since yesterday?" I asked
as guilt set in. I should've been with my son before
he was called to Heaven. I should've been the one
here at the hospital all day. But instead, I was
locked up behind King's bullshit. The more I
thought about things, the angrier I was becoming.

"Yes baby, I've been sitting right here." She

paused to blow her nose. "I just couldn't leave him, Jasmine. I couldn't leave him all alone in there by himself." She cried and pointed to the window behind us. "Jordan was such a good boy; I just wish his dad had given him a chance."

The words that she spoke made my blood boil because it was absolutely true. Instead of loving and caring for our son, King treated him like he was nothing and didn't matter. "Mama, what am I going to do now? My only reason for breathing was Jordan and God took him from me!" I was mad at the world, including the Lord himself. Dammit! I was a good person. I did nice things for people and spoke kind words to everyone. So why would this happen to me? "Mama, you know the Lord right?" My nostrils flared. "Ask Him why He did this! Didn't God know that I needed my son in order to survive? Without Jordan, I'm dead! You might as well bury me too!" I declared.

"Jasmine, you stop that, you hear me? God will never put more on us than we can bear. Do you understand that, baby?" She rubbed my back as I released all of my pain, tears, and frustration. "The Lord loaned Jordan to us for four beautiful years, but he was ready for *His* son to come home. You are a great mom and you always will be a wonderful person. This had nothing to do with you. Jordan's life, no matter how short, was predestined and it was God's will for him to go home." My mother was right but I couldn't help the way I was feeling. I just prayed that God would understand.

I laid my head down on my mother's lap as she rocked me like an infant. So many thoughts ran through my mind that my head began to throb. I was a ball of emotions; I couldn't stop the pain. I felt hurt, angry, upset, betrayed, and lonely. "Jasmine, do you want to see Jordan before the funeral home comes to pick him up?"

"No mama. You go ahead, I can't." Shaking my head, I stood up from the blue, plastic, chair and went to get some air. On my way outside, I called King.

"Yeah?"

"King, it's Jordan. He died baby; our son is

gone." I cried hysterically.

"Stop, I'm on the phone…you play too much." He said to some girl that was giggling in the background. "Jasmine, you said what?" King asked and I rolled my eyes.

"I said our son is fucking dead!" I snapped, causing several people to stop and stare at me.

"Damn, I'm sorry to hear that. Are you okay; do you need anything?" He asked like a friend of the family would. *Didn't he realize Jordan was his son too?*

"Yes King, I do need something. I need you to be here! You've never been there for your son during his whole life, can't you at least make him a priority now that he's gone!?" I screamed into the receiver.

"Chill the fuck out with that yelling! I'll be home tomorrow and I'll see you then!" He snarled.

"So you telling me a muthafuckin music video is more important than your son?" I was fuming.

"I ain't saying all that Jasmine, but this is

how I get paid. Somebody gotta make the money to pay for his funeral, right?" He barked and I stood speechless. "That's what I thought! Like I said, I'll be home tomorrow." Click!

Chapter Thirty-one
Tionne

As Zuri slept peacefully in my hotel bed, I
had quietly grabbed the keys to my car which
hadn't been repossessed yet and exited the room.
We had planned to go over to her house and collect
her things later this evening but I wasn't stupid. We
needed protection and I knew just where to get it.
Dallas and I both had our license to carry concealed
weapons as well as an arsenal of firearms, so I
headed home, a place I never thought I would see
again.

Within twenty minutes, I was pulling up to
the gate and punching in the code. I halfway
expected that Dallas had changed it as well as the
locks, but like magic, the doors parted like the red
sea. Pulling into the large driveway, I noticed that
Dallas's car was gone and I exhaled. His not being
here really made my task a lot easier. It would also
give me a chance to grab some of the shit I
should've grabbed when I initially left, before I

found out I was broke. Truthfully, I was a tad homesick and the sight of my mansion made me miss everything about my old life. It was nice to live carefree, even if I had to deal with a few bitches here and there. Zuri's situation made me realize that I didn't have it that bad. *Maybe Dallas and I could work it out and seek counseling?* I thought to myself before remembering the dreaded call from the doctor's office. *What if it was AIDS?* The conversation I remembered having not long ago with Zuri played in my head.

Shaking off my thoughts, I stepped from the whip and proceeded to the door. After sliding my key into the lock, I prayed it worked which it did. Once inside the house, I flew to the alarm panel. Surprisingly, it wasn't armed. "Just like Dallas to be so careless." I mumbled before turning to face the mess of clothes, pizza boxes, and other shit thrown all over the place. "Some things never change." Dallas had really been partying in my absence. Lori, the maid was going to go ape shit when she saw this place. It would take her two days to get it right and get the smell of feet and old food out of the furniture.

Remembering the task at hand, I hurriedly ran through the house searching for the key to the gun cabinet that was sitting along the wall of our family room. It wasn't in the kitchen drawer, or the desk drawer in Dallas's office. That's when I remembered he had moved the key up to our bedroom where he kept it in the nightstand. Taking them two by two, I made it up the stairs to our room door, which was closed. Without hesitation, I barged right in. What I saw next, had my mouth dragging the floor. Dallas was naked in bed with not one but two people–both of them were men.

When the shock of what I was seeing finally wore off, I removed my cell phone and did the first thing that came to mind–I started snapping pictures like the paparazzi. Realizing photos of Dallas spooning a man and holding his waist while another sandwiched him were priceless, I was sure to get one from every angle. One of the men began to stir. I almost pissed myself when I saw Gangsta Grizzly, a notorious west coast rapper known for being a bully in the industry. "What the fuck!" He began tapping the others to wake them up. Thinking fast, I grabbed the key from the nightstand and flew downstairs to the gun cabinet.

No sooner than I had two Smith and Wesson's in hand did Dallas bring his gay ass down the stairs. "Tionne, what are you doing?" He asked like I hadn't just caught him in bed with two dudes.

"Securing my future!" I snapped.

"What?"

"Yeah buddy, you and your friends are going to pay big time for the fun you had last night. I want twenty million dollars in my account by tomorrow or these pictures get leaked.

"You wouldn't dare." Dallas tried to come for me but I let off a warning shot to back him up. He knew from days at the gun range that my precision with a weapon was deadly. Therefore, he dared not make a move.

"The tabloids would probably pay twice as much. As a matter of fact, I might just call them." I slowly backed toward the door.

"Alright, you got it. Twenty mill in your account tomorrow." Dallas had his hands raised in surrender.

"I want one mill from big man too." I nodded to Grizzly who was at the top of the stairs. He wasn't worth nearly as much as my husband. One million was probably all he had.

"Whatever you want, it's yours." Dallas gritted his teeth. "Just give me the phone."

"You'll get the phone when I get the money." Tucking one of the guns under my arm, I unlocked the door then hauled ass to my car.

Chapter Thirty-two
Zuri

After awaking from my power nap, I had to hit the ground running in Tionne's absence. As much as I wanted to wait for her, I knew my window of opportunity was small. Jason would be home in less than three hours. Therefore, I had to get going. "Shit." I said, suddenly remembering that I didn't have a car. Thinking fast, I grabbed my phone and dialed Lyric.

"Hey, this is your girl Lyric. I'm unavailable at the moment. Leave me a message and I'll call you back as soon I'm able. Have a great day and remember that I love you."

"Hey Lyric, it's me. I was calling you for a ride. If you're free, call me back. Love you too girl." I ended the call with a smile. My girl Lyric was a firm believer in saying she loved you at the end of every call to all her family and friends. I used to think it was strange before she explained her reasoning.

"Girl, people don't last forever so you never want to miss the opportunity to say I love you."

Lyric was the reason I now said it as well.

After calling Tionne twice, I finally gave up and grabbed the hotel phone to dial out. "Front Desk. This is Sarah."

"Hi Sarah, can you please call a metro car for me." I said while slipping into my shoes.

"There is actually one out front already."

"Good! I'll be right down." Grabbing my purse from the desktop, I ended the call and flew out the door.

The entire ride home had me nervous and sick to my stomach. There were so many questions weighing heavy on my mind that it was becoming hard to think. I knew I was making the best decision for myself and Jelly but somehow, I didn't feel right about it. I felt like a criminal sneaking into my own home, stealing my belongings, and ultimately kidnapping my daughter. Speaking of Jelly, I wondered how my actions would affect her. It wasn't fair to keep her away from Jason but right now, I had to do what I had to do.

"Mrs., I said we're here." The driver of the metro car sat idling in my driveway. "Would you like me to wait for you?"

"Um no; I'm good." I said before handing him a twenty dollar tip. The bill for the service had been added to the account we already had with them.

"Have a good day." The driver said as I stepped out and closed the door.

Just as I approached the door, it popped open and I jumped. "Hi, Mrs. Armstrong. I wasn't expecting you back for a few days." Helen, the nanny greeted me with a smile. She was holding Jelly who immediately reached for me when she saw me.

"There was a change of plans." I took hold of my daughter and kissed her soft lips. "Where is Sylvia?"

"She just left for her daily walk around the neighborhood." Helen closed the door and followed me into the house.

"I need you to take Jelly upstairs to get dressed. Then go to the MKX in the garage and strap her in. Stay with her in the car until I come out there, okay." I kissed Jelly once more before handing her over.

"Yes ma'am." Helen didn't ask any questions, which I liked about her. She simply nodded her understanding then flew up the stairs. I raced up behind her as fast as I could. My side was still hurting but the adrenaline racing through my veins had me going.

The minute I hit the top step, I entered my bedroom and went over to my side of the bed. After lifting the sheets, I ran my hand along the edges until I found the slit I'd cut years ago. It was one of my hiding spots that housed a few stacks of money. Hastily, I retrieved what was in there and tossed them on top of the bed. Next, I went over to the closet and grabbed two Dooney & Burke duffle bags. One of them was empty, the other served as another one of my hiding spots. It too was filled partially with money. One thing I learned a long time ago was to not trust the bank with all of your dough. After tossing the money on the bed into the bag, I took both bags into my daughter's room. Helen had just finished putting her shoes on. Jelly was trying to eat them while sitting in her car seat. "Helen, can you take her stroller downstairs for me?"

"Yes ma'am."

"Thank you." I nodded before grabbing all of Jelly's diapers, wipes, toys, and a few articles of clothing then tossing them in the empty bag. Glancing down at my watch, I was making good time or so I thought until I heard the front door open and Helen address Jason. "Fuck!" Right at this moment, I could've passed out but I knew if I stopped now I'd be here forever.

"Zuri." The sound of Jason calling my name locked my bowels up instantly.

Without responding, I zipped up the bag, grabbed the other one and Jelly's car seat in one swift motion. "Didn't you hear me calling you?"

"No, I didn't." I replied before turning to

face him.

"When did you come back? What happened?" Jason walked into the room then stood behind me.

"Tionne left her passport and Lyric never showed up." Finally, I turned around slowly.

"Where are you going? He looked down at the bags and the car seat.

"Well I thought I would take Jelly to spend a few nights with aunt T." I lied with a straight face. "She's been having a tough time lately and was really looking forward to our girl time."

"You must think I'm stupid." Jason's jowl muscle clinched. "I saw you on the surveillance tape packing your money." WHAP! With a closed fist, my husband rocked my face sending me stumbling backwards. I'd completely forgotten about the nearly invisible cameras we had throughout our home. "Are you leaving me?"

"Yes Jason. I'm leaving and I'm never coming back. Fuck you and your money!" I tried to barge past him but he caught me a left hook then a right. Losing my balance, I dropped both of the duffle bags and Jelly's car seat to the floor then hit the floor myself. Just as Jason lifted his right foot to kick me, I crawled over to his left leg and bit him so hard that I'm sure I drew blood.

"Bitch!" He kneeled down to check out his leg. When he did, I snatched the lamp off the table near the rocking chair where I sometimes read to Jelly and broke it across his face.

By now, Jason was seething but I'd brought enough time to stand to my feet, grab Jelly, one duffle bag, and make it into the hallway. "You will never leave me Zuri!" Jason yelled from the bedroom.

"Fuck you! I'm done." Although my body was weak, my feet kept moving toward the staircase.

"The only way you're leaving is in a body bag. Do you hear me?" Jason was now in the hallway behind me. "Do you hear me…in a fucking body bag!" He flew toward me just as I looked back. The fury in his eyes had replaced the brown pupils I once knew to be kind and gentle. My husband was possessed and completely unaware of what he was doing when he tackled me at the exact time that I approached the edge of the stairs.

"No!" Sylvia screamed from the foyer.

I felt myself falling and watched in slow motion as she and Helen covered their eyes in horror when Jelly and I both went tumbling down the spiral staircase with force. Desperately, I tried to protect my daughter as she screamed for dear life but there was nothing I could do. BOOM. BANG. BOOM. The sound of my head hitting the hard tile was loud enough for me to know that I was bleeding and hurt pretty bad. THUD! Finally, my body reached the foyer. By then, I couldn't see, hear, or move.

Chapter Thirty-three
Jasmine

Just as I was about to call him back, my cell phone vibrated, it was Stacey. "Bitch, don't ever call my muthafuckin phone again in life!" I warned.

"What did I do to you?" She asked. "I should be the one mad; I ain't heard from you in two weeks."

"And you won't ever hear from me again once we end this phone call with your phony ass."

"Phony? Please! I'm the realest bitch you know." Stacey stated matter-of-factly.

"You were the realest bitch I knew up until you let your stank ass sister fuck my husband and make two babies." I bit down on my bottom lip until I tasted blood.

"Wait a minute, what?" She played dumb.

"Don't act like you didn't know Stacey. Just woman up and tell the truth." I hailed one of the cabs lingering by the curb. I needed to leave this hospital and fast.

"Look," she sighed. "I knew they fucked once way back in the day before he got locked up but I swear I didn't know they started messing around again."

"Fuck messing around, I could get over that shit!" I told her. "That bitch had his babies and that ain't cool Stacey. When I see your sister, I'ma fuck her up on sight. I would advise you not to jump in if you don't want to get fucked up too!" I warned her and I meant it. When I faced off with Tracey, I wanted it to be one-on-one, but if Stacey jumped in, I had something for her ass too.

"Are you sure those are his kids? They don't even look like him." She was right; they didn't look like him. They looked dead like their mom but I knew it had to be true if King was claiming them.

"King, Prince, and Princess...do you get it now?" I said pulling the phone away from my face to give the cab driver my address. "You ain't got shit to say about that, huh?" I put the phone back up to my ear.

"Jasmine, I'm so very sorry," was the best

she could come up with.

"Well save your sorry; I've had more than my share of sorry for this lifetime." I wiped at the silent tears slipping down my face. "I'm sorry that you're a snake! I'm sorry that your sister is a slut! I'm sorry that my husband ain't shit and I'm fuckin' sorry that my son had to die!"

"Die? Jasmine, what do you mean he had to die?" She was confused.

"Die, as in dead! My son didn't fucking wake up yesterday afternoon." I got choked up.

"Oh my God! Where are you? I'm on my way!"

"Please stay the fuck away from me." I urged and ended the call. I wasn't in the best mental space at the moment. Therefore, I needed time to myself. I hoped she would respect my wishes and leave me alone, especially for her own safety. With all the pent-up anger and rage in my heart, I was liable to do anything.

Thirty minutes later, the cab pulled up to my gate. I paid the driver, punched the code in, and walked up my circular driveway in silence. Taking in the scenery acre by acre, I surveyed the house that I used to love so much. I had only been gone for a day but everything looked different–sort of foreign. Placing my key into the front door, I paused, took a deep breath then turned the key. It felt out of place to be there and I was extremely uneasy. I ran up the stairs into my bedroom. Rummaging through my belongings like a mad woman, I raced around the room packing all of my sentimental items. I packed a few pieces of clothing, grabbed about two pairs of shoes, and all of mine and Jordan's personal documents. Yesterday, I had a plan to take it all. Today, I just wanted to leave with what I had come here with.

I pulled my wedding ring and band off, placing them both on King's nightstand. I headed downstairs to the garage but stopped in my tracks as the large, oil painting of me holding Jordan when he was a baby caught my attention. We had taken it when he was two months old and I adored it. The inscription on the bottom of the gold frame made

me cry as I read it aloud, *"There is an enduring tenderness in the love of a mother to a son that transcends all other affections of the heart."*
-*Washington Irving*

Wiping my eyes, I reached up and removed it from the wall. This would be my way of taking a piece of my son with me.

Just as I loaded up the Navigator, my cell phone rang. "Didn't I tell you to leave me the hell alone?" I snapped because I figured it was Stacey.

"Where did you go baby?" My mama asked full of concern.

"Oh mama, I'm sorry. I thought you were Stacey. I had to come home and get a few things. I'm sorry but I couldn't stay at that hospital." I apologized.

"I understand baby. Well did you get ahold of King?"

"Yes ma'am I did but you already know how that went." I smacked my lips as my line beeped. "Mama, I'm on my way to your house. I'll see you in a few minutes, okay." I said and clicked over.

"Hello?" I waited for someone to respond. I glanced at the caller ID; it was a private call. "Who the fuck is this?" I got into the driver's seat then pulled away from the garage.

"It's the bitch that's fucking your man." The caller said.

"So this must be Tracey's stank ass or one of his other baby mamas." I cut into her and she smacked her lips.

"So how does it feel to know you got played? I been fucking him the whole time y'all been together." She beamed.

"You and every bitch he comes in contact with." I laughed but she didn't.

"Anyway Jasmine, I was just calling to let you know that your man been with me the last two days. He ain't at no damn video shoot. His ass been laying next to me like he always do when he tells you he's out-of-town."

"If y'all been playing house and he's been lying about being out-of-town, why you calling to let me know now? I parked the truck and waited for her answer.

"Because King is finally going to leave you."

"Good, because I'm sick of him anyway! Congrats and best wishes." I said, reaching to tap the end button on my phone.

"He was going to leave you after you had Jordan." Tracey blurted out. "He said it was bad for his image to have a child with special needs. Plus, his publicist, Danielle, told him not to."

"Keep my son's name out of your mouth." I advised.

"Nevertheless, now that your son is gone, me, him, and our kids can finally be a family."

"Tracey, don't mention my son again if you want to live and see another day." I would kill this hoe in a heart beat and that's a promise.

"What you gon' do?" She tried me.

"Tracey, don't test my gangsta!"

"Anyway Jasmine, have a nice life! You ain't got no son, no husband, and you won't have no money because I bet your dumb ass signed a prenuptial agreement." She laughed. "You might as well go kill yourself."

"Actually, that's not a bad idea." I agreed, causing her to fall silent. She was wrong about me signing a prenup. Actually, I was entitled to half of everything King owned. However, she was right about me being alone. Without Jordan, neither the money nor the possessions meant a thing to me. What did I have to look forward to in the morning? Nothing! So why not off myself? Hell, if I was going out, why not take King and his mistress with me? I laughed hysterically, making Tracey uneasy.

I hung up on Tracey who I'm sure was freaking out right now and called the cell phone company. "Hello Mrs. James, what can I do for you today?" Stephanie, my personal Sprint representative, asked. She was assigned to us when King became famous. She handled our account personally and kept our records confidential from the public and other Sprint employees.

"Hey Stephanie, King lost his phone. We need to either find it or have it turned off. We think its still here at the hotel in the room we're staying in, so I wanted you to check the GPS tracking device for me." I lied but I needed to know where King was.

"Mrs. James, you're right. The phone is still at the Dell Hotel; I show that it was last active about thirty minutes ago." She confirmed.

"Thanks Stephanie, have a good one." I smiled and ended the call. His ass was just up the street from our house; how convenient.

I ran back into the house and into King's study. I used the small key on the key ring to unlock the bottom drawer of his desk. Staring back at me was a nickel-plated nine millimeter. Without hesitation, I reached for it. After checking for bullets, I dropped it into my purse and hopped back into my SUV, leaving my front door wide-open. I felt myself losing it and tried to reason with my alter ego all the way over to the hotel. Unfortunately, she wasn't having it. This was her breaking point and I could do nothing to stop her.

Pulling into the parking lot on two wheels, I

put the SUV in park, and hopped out right at the door.

"Thank you for visiting the Dell; how can I help you?" A young, African American girl asked with a bucktooth smile as large as Texas.

"Hey Shanika." I looked at her gold name tag. My husband, King James, is here and I need to know what room." I wasn't trying to pretend anymore, so I didn't have to make up a story with her.

"Um, I can't give out that information, ma'am."

"Will this help you?" I placed five hundred dollars on top of the black countertop. Nervously, she looked from side to side before sliding the money toward her. Then she tapped on the keyboard then looked up at me.

"Room 616," she whispered.

Chapter Thirty-four

Jasmine

I tried to talk myself out of what I was about to do but it wasn't working. My mind was on overload with everything on my plate. I stepped from the elevator and pulled the gun from my purse. A couple passed me in the hallway and gasped, but I no longer cared or had control over my actions. It was at this moment that I realized how people snapped and claimed temporary insanity. I was going to do what I came here for and it didn't matter to me if I left in handcuffs or a body bag.

Knock! Knock! I banged on the door.

"Who is that knocking like the police?" I heard King say.

"You go ahead and shower; I'll get it baby." Tracey called back to him as she swung the door open. "What the hell?"

"Room service bitch!" I pushed my nickel-plated nine up against her chest and forced my way into the hotel suite.

"It's like that, Jasmine?" She asked while trying to cover her butt-naked ass.

"Yeah bitch, it's definitely like that!"

BOOM. I pulled the trigger without a second thought. Tracey stumbled a few times, finally falling backwards, shattering the glass, coffee table. I walked up and stood over her. "See what fucking my husband got you?" I asked. "Now you tell me if it was worth it?"

"Please." She barely whispered as she gurgled blood around in her throat.

"Please what? Speak up; I can't hear you?" I taunted. "You thought you were big shit over the phone, didn't you?" BANG. I shot her trifling ass again as an afterthought. King flew from the bathroom with a white towel wrapped around his waist.

"Jasmine, what the fuck?" Was all he said before I aimed the gun at him.

"I was the last person you expected to see today right?" I asked. "Your lying ass was here laid up this whole time with this bitch. You were less than twenty minutes away from the hospital and couldn't come and say goodbye to your son?" I wagged my finger, "Bad move!"

"Jasmine, I was working." He continued to lie.

"You call this work? Yeah right! This is some video set." I faked a smile and he shifted nervously. "You must've been making a porno instead of a music video." I laughed wickedly as I scanned the room with disgust. There were several shopping bags, liquor bottles, and condom wrappers scattered throughout the room. These two mofos was up in here fuckin' and living it up while I was in jail, and my son was lying in the morgue.

"Jasmine, let me explain." He pleaded like a bitch.

"Ain't shit to explain, King. The writing is on the wall and you gave it to me straight the other night, remember." I stepped over Tracey's dead body and walked toward my husband.

"Put the gun down." King begged.

"Or what? What are you gonna do, hit me?"

311

I dared him to make a move. The minute he moved
an inch, I was busting a cap in his ass.

"Jasmine, you don't really want to hurt me,
do you?" He asked like this was a game.

"Why not? You've hurt me plenty of times.
Over and over, you continued to treat me like the
shit on the bottom of your shoe." I stepped forward
which made King so nervous that he let go of the
towel, raising both his hands in the air. The sight of
his shriveled up dick made me sick to my stomach.
POP! I had aimed right between his legs and blew
his dick off, balls and all.

"Oh shit!" King dropped down to his knees,
rolling around on the floor in pain.

"Guess you won't be making any more
babies, huh?" I went and bent down beside him.
"That shit hurts like hell, doesn't it?"

"Why you doing this?"

"Because I'm sick and tired of your bullshit.
I've come to the end of my rope and you've come
to the end of the road." I stood right over him with
my gun pointed at his head.

"What you saying, Jas?" King looked scared shitless.

"I'm saying that you better make peace 'cause you're about to meet your maker." I pressed the gun to the middle of his forehead.

"You going to hell, Jasmine; do you hear me?" King cried.

"Then I guess I'll see you at the crossroads so you won't be lonely." I sung the Bone Thugs in Harmony lyric. POP!

I can't explain it but I wasn't scared or remorseful for what I'd just done. In fact, I felt vindicated and relieved. My nerves were calm, my heart rate was steady, and I felt like a new woman. I picked up the hotel's cordless phone and walked into the bathroom. Staring at my reflection in the mirror, I no longer saw a woman dying to be loved and appreciated. No, the reflection staring back at me was that of a warrior, a fighter, an independent woman with no more tears! Dialing 911, I smiled at the new me.

"911, what's the emergency?" A chipper

operator answered the call.

"I would like to report a double homicide."

"Excuse me, but did you say you're calling to report a double homicide?" The operator asked for clarification.

"Yes! Two people are dead." I said calmly.

"What's your location?"

"I'm at the Dell Hotel inside room 616." I answered.

"Okay, stay calm. Police and emergency medical units have been dispatched. Help is on the way!" The operator sounded alarmed. "Are you in any danger?"

"No. Not anymore." I replied feeling the safest I'd felt in a very long time.

"Is the assailant still on the premises? Is he or she nearby?"

"Yes, she's here. As a matter of fact, she's so close, I can touch her." I said while placing the palm of my hand against the mirror.

"I'm going to stay on the phone with you until help arrives." She conveyed.

"Help better get here fast before there's one more body added to the number." Dropping the phone into the sink, I placed the gun to my head, prepared to take what was left of my life.

Before I could pull the trigger, I was bum rushed by two, male, police officers. "Put the gun down!" One of them yelled as the other one snatched it from my hand. Once again, I was placed under arrest and handcuffed. I guess someone heard the gunshots or the couple in the hallway must've called the police because they showed up extremely fast.

"Aww shit! That's KJ, the famous rapper from Independent Records." The young, black cop stated for the other cop to hear.

"Damn, she blew his dick off." The young, white cop confirmed after getting a closer look. He sat me down on the bed then pulled out his cell phone to take a few pictures of the bloody crime scene.

"I'm 'bout to get paid." He laughed along with his partner.

"Yeah, I heard Sloppy Gossip magazine pays top notch for shit like this." The black guy pulled out his phone as well and followed suit. This foolishness went on for another twenty minutes as I sat and waited to be taken to jail.

"Damn shorty, what these people do to you?" The black cop asked.

"More than you can imagine," was my reply.

"It must've been pretty messed up for you to go this far. You don't even look like the type to do some stuff like this. This right here is just cold-blooded." The white cop added as he helped me stand from the bed then walked me toward the door.

"You do realize that you just flushed all your fame and fortune down the drain, right?" The black officer asked. I stopped dead in my tracks, looked back at Tracey then at King for the last time.

"I guess when a woman's fed up, fame and fortune don't mean shit!"

THE END

ABOUT THE AUTHOR

India Williams is a 27-year-old national best-selling author of two series, The Real Hoodwives of Detroit and Gangstress. Born and raised in Detroit, Michigan, India attended Wayne State University. She majored in business management and minored in secondary education.

Writing and language arts have always been her favorite subjects. She wrote her first story in the sixth grade and received tons of support from family as well as teachers. In 2010, she found the courage to pen her first novel, "Dope, Death, and Deception." Instantly, it became a hit within the urban community.

Embracing her entrepreneurial spirit, since then, India has created her own publishing company, "Grade A Publications," penned ten novels in total, and contributed her literary talent to four anthologies.

Just Released
On The Run
(short novella) by India

COMING SOON
The Real Hoodwives of Detroit 4 by India

If you have a manuscript you would like us to review,

email us today at Gradeapub@gmail.com.

Grade A Publications Order Form

(All books are $13.00, which includes shipping.)

Name:

Address:

City: _____ State: _____ Zip:

QTY _____ Dope, Death, & Deception   Total: _____

QTY _____ Still Deceiving   Total: _____

QTY _____ The Real Hoodwives of Detroit 1   Total: _____

QTY _____ Money Over Everything   Total: _____

QTY _____ The Real Hoodwives of Detroit 2   Total: _____

QTY _____ The Real Hoodwives of Detroit 3   Total: _____

QTY _____ Gangstress 1   Total: _____

QTY _____ Gangstress 2   Total: _____

QTY _____ Celebrity Wives Association   Total: _____

TOTAL: $_____

Please Send All Order Forms And Money Orders To:

GRADE A PUBLICATIONS
P.O BOX 18175
FAIRFIELD, OHIO 45018

Ayeshia

Made in the USA
Middletown, DE
03 April 2023

28176327R00191